About the author

Steinunn Sigurðardóttir (Iceland, 1950) is a highly acclaimed Icelandic novelist and poet. After working as a journalist and radio reporter she became a full-time writer in 1982. As one of the most frequently translated living Icelandic writers, she has contributed greatly to the international reputation of contemporary Icelandic literature. Steinunn Sigurðardóttir has served on the jury of the IMPAC Dublin Literary Award and as vice-chair of the Icelandic Writers' Association. Her novel *Yo-yo* was awarded the Icelandic Bookseller's award and has been translated into German and French. In 2015 the Dutch translation will be published.

About the translator

Rory McTurk, Professor Emeritus of Icelandic Studies at the University of Leeds, is a translator of Old and Modern Icelandic poetry and prose, and the author of books and articles on Icelandic and related literature. His translation of Steinunn Sigurðardóttir's novel *The Thief of Time* was published in 2007.

Yo-yo

Steinunn Sigurðardóttir

Yo-yo

Translated from the Icelandic
by Rory McTurk

World Editions

Published in Great Britain in 2015 by World Editions Ltd., London

www.worldeditions.org

Copyright © Steinunn Sigurðardóttir, 2011
English translation copyright © Rory McTurk and
World Editions, 2015
Cover design Multitude

First published as *jójó* in Iceland in 2011 by Bjartur, Reykjavík

British Library Cataloguing-in-Publication Data
A catalogue record for this book is available on request
from the British Library

ISBN 978-94-6238-053-0

Typeset in Minion Pro

This book has been translated with financial support
from the Icelandic Literature Center

MIÐSTÖÐ ÍSLENSKRA BÓKMENNTA
ICELANDIC LITERATURE CENTER

Distribution Europe (except the Netherlands and Belgium):
Turnaround Publishers Services, London
Distribution the Netherlands and Belgium: Centraal Boekhuis,
Culemborg, the Netherlands

This book is dedicated
to Hlín Agnarsdóttir

'WHY ME?' HE whimpers, from the other side of my desk: 'Why should I, of all people, have to suffer this?'

I should have given him an appointment on Monday, as planned. Now I'm stuck with him at eighteen minutes past three with the end of the working day nowhere in sight. I long to be outside on this beautiful spring day with my beloved Petra, relaxing under a five-tiered canopy of chestnut blossom and having a beer—or perhaps some of that rosé wine from Provence that Martin gave me a taste for.

'Why me in particular?' he persists.

Just because, mate; it's the statistics of 'just because'. But I can't say that out loud, so I trot out my doctor-to-patient speech:

'One person in every three gets cancer at some stage of their lives. We can't say for certain why a particular person gets a particular form of it. There are of course risk factors: smoking, obesity, heavy drinking, sedentary lifestyle…'

'But none of those apply in my case. I lead a very healthy life, my food's organic—eighty-five to ninety per cent organic—I watch my waist line' (he rips off his black jacket and drums with his fingers on his stomach)—'and I go for long walks around the town, six times a week at least, two to three hours at a time, and still this happens to me; why me?'

'You should bear in mind that there are many kinds of cancer, of varying degrees of seriousness, and with varying prospects of recovery. Your case doesn't look half bad; your chances are good, as we've told you.'

'But in the oesophagus! That's about as bad as it can get.'

'We never know where it's going to strike.'

'I just don't understand,' he says, his voice breaking, 'why it had to happen to me.'

'Your chances are good,' I repeat. I pass him a Kleenex and start explaining the treatment I've devised—perhaps not in strict accord with what the chemo quacks originally recommended, but I've reached the stage where I generally get my own way without too much opposition. I'm known for finding the best way forward when it comes to treatment.

It's tempting to explain to a patient who reacts like this how much less fortunate he could be, and that there are much worse conditions than his particular one, but it's a temptation one has to resist, in the interests of professionalism. The oesophagus is an awkward place, it's true, but it's only a small tumour and unlikely to hold out against my style of therapy. It hasn't spread, and we've told the patient straight out that it's curable (though one can't of course sign a guarantee to that effect), and there he sits, whining, a neatly turned out, soft-spoken man of seventy-three.

I've had really young people in that chair to whom I've given the worst possible news, and they've accepted it like

any other inescapable fact of life, without batting an eyelid, and asking practical questions about treatment and
side effects: whether they would live for three months, six
months or a year, and whether it would be better to die
from the disease itself or from the treatment, if they had
the choice. More than one of these dear patients of mine
lived longer than expected, and two are still alive, both of
them now two years past the date I gave them when they
pressed me for an answer.

I don't normally give patients a date, unless they press
me. It seems cruel: as if I'm setting up as a prophet in pos-
session of divine powers. Time prognosis is unscientific,
imprecise, and can sometimes be harmful. It's happened
more than once that a patient has died before the date I
gave him, and those were patients I thought could live for
at least two or three months. One died within a week and
the other in ten days, which meant that they didn't have
the time they thought they had, poor devils, to say their
goodbyes and put their affairs in order.

This patient is still blubbering about how difficult the
treatment's going to be, how he may die in any case, and
whether he can be sure of not losing his hair—and this
from a man who's half bald anyway! He raises his hands,
the backs of which are hairy enough, to the crown of his
head, where there's not a hair to be seen.

My patience is running out. I count up to ten and point
out that one thing he can be thankful for is not having an

operation, and that patients respond to the treatment in different ways. The particular cocktail of drugs and rays he's going to have is generally easy to tolerate. The likeliest side effects are tiredness and indigestion.

'That'll be hard to take; I have a weak stomach.'

'It'll sort itself out. You're in good shape generally.'

'Well, I do look after myself.'

'That can only be a good thing.'

I had thought of giving him a quick once-over, as I usually do at the first consultation, checking the lymph nodes in the armpits, neck and groin, but there's no need. It's not as if my colleagues haven't examined him already, from all angles.

And in any case our conversation has run well over time; my last patient of the day must have been waiting for at least three quarters of an hour.

'I'm here in this building, where you'll be coming for your radiotherapy, so I'm easy to get hold of.'

'Thank God for that. I'm clearly in the hands of a first-rate doctor.'

'Let's hope so.'

He smiles unexpectedly. An unctuous smile, completely out of keeping with the clean-shaven, well-groomed man before me, in his funereally black jacket.

He shows no sign of going and is about to say something else.

I stand up, in the hope that he'll leave.

The patient says goodbye, still lingering. Then he comes up and claps me on the shoulder, with an air of condescension. There's something familiar about his back view as he walks towards the door, recalling someone from my far-distant past. A teacher at primary school, perhaps? Someone in a shop?

Curiosity compels me to open the door for him, and there in the corridor is a woman who's been waiting for him. That's unusual: the next-of-kin, if there is one, usually comes to see me with the patient, especially at the first consultation.

His wife, as I take her to be, stands up stiffly. She looks ten years older than he does. She's a grey individual, from all points of view: hair, skin colour, clothes. Her shoes, too, are a dusty grey.

The woman looks down at the floor as if to make quite sure she's standing on terra firma. The man strides past her. I'm astonished to see him moving so fast after the way he dragged his feet in the consulting room.

The woman totters after him to the end of the corridor like the fluttering shadow of a branch in the wind. 'With a walk like the walk of the dead,' as Martin once said of a Catalan he made friends with in the gutter, and now I see what that could have looked like. The back view of the man continues to nag at me: that walk, that military step. It annoys me that I can't place him. What's happened to Martin Montag's marvellous memory?

THE AIR'S HEAVY in my room even though the window is half open. I open it all the way and take a lungful of fresh air. Now I've just got to grit my teeth and finish the day's tasks swiftly and surely, leaving till tomorrow the few things that can be left, so that I can get away with alacrity to join Petra under the canopy of chestnut blossom: out into the long-awaited spring, the spring which delayed its coming, but then came with such a vengeance that the chestnut blossoms were out earlier than anyone can remember.

The tumour in this patient's oesophagus (the second-last patient of the day!) appears unexpectedly on the screen when I touch the mouse. It's a round-shaped tumour and fiery-red, too, as it appears on the screen. Its location is fortunate: it'll be relatively easy to attack it with radiation without doing too much harm to the healthy tissues. It's a small tumour, just about a centimetre in diameter. It's a fast-growing one, too, easier to deal with than one of those slow tumours, which sounds like a contradiction and often surprises patients. But there's something about this round excrescence that suggests to me that it's hiding something. The fact that the patient in question comes across as a whiner doesn't help. Unless there's more to him, too, than meets the eye, as one might think from that unexpected, unctuous smile, and from the way he strode to the end of the passage with that shadow of a wife behind him, having behaved with me like someone who could do little more than crawl on all fours.

A tumour sometimes has the same sort of personality as the person it attacks. And sometimes it has a totally different character from the person it seeks to destroy. You could find a small and especially malignant tumour hidden slyly away in the tallest and most affable of men.

A small, round, fast-growing tumour, looking like a bright red yo-yo: how does that square with such a prim and proper, self-pitying exterior? With someone whose greatest worry is that the treatment may make him bald, when he's half bald already?

IT'S NO EASY matter bringing the day to an end. My concentration has gone. I open all the windows as wide as I can, but the air is still as thick and claustrophobic as a brick wall. I open the door, but the through-draught makes no difference. I'm even breathing with difficulty, as though my heart's playing up.

It would cause something of a sensation if a thirty-four-year-old runner-cum-doctor had a heart attack and died suddenly, though such cases are not unknown. If it's going to happen to me now I'd rather do my dying out in the spring sunshine than in the consulting room, even if the sun is streaming in through the open windows and dancing on the walls.

I throw my white coat over the back of a chair, and find

myself having to acknowledge a nagging pain of some sort in my left upper arm. Martin Montag, as I see him in the mirror, is pale-faced and sweating. It's some time since I last looked in the mirror, and my beard now looks like that of a savage. What's happening to the man in the mirror? Is he ageing extra-fast? The curve on that sweating, aquiline nose is now surely higher up than before, and there's a film over those eyes which Petra says are usually green and clear. Eyes that shine in the dark, she says, like an animal's!

I hurry down the stairs by the roundabout route and out through the back door, the doctor's escape route when he needs to get away without encumbrance. But I'm not altogether unobserved even now: that big woman with cancer of the salivary gland is coming out of radiotherapy and has also chosen this little-used means of exit.

I REALLY ADMIRE my patients: seeing them sitting there, uncomplaining, in that bleak, windowless waiting room, waiting for radiotherapy, day after day if they're unlucky, for one hour, two hours, or longer. And some have to wait every bit as long after treatment if they're dependent on hospital transport. Elderly, infirm, weighed down with exhaustion, and not showing the least sign of it: self-pity is not the order of the day here. So it's all the more surprising to encounter it in such blatant form as in my second-last patient today. I don't like that man, and for me this is un-usual: normally I like my patients.

There's always a particular one I regard as my favourite. This time it's the big woman with cancer of the mouth: she had to have her teeth out. My heart bled for her, losing her teeth on top of everything else. It was a bit of nuisance, she said, but at least it gave scope for some leg-pulling about toothlessness with the man she lived with. You wouldn't think there was anything special about this woman, one way or the other, but I've never seen anything quite like the way she copes with illness and therapy. You can't even call it stoicism. She accepts things as a matter of course: too much so. She asks too few questions. It's almost as if her problem doesn't concern her. She's one of those people who don't want fuss, even in matters of life and death.

She's embarrassed when I greet her with open arms in the waiting room. She didn't know how to react when it was clear to her at the first consultation that her case was one of particular concern to me.

IT'S A LONG way to go, given that I want to bring a speedy end to the day, but I hasten to the bench on which Martin and I used to sit by the summer house in the western-most part of the hospital complex. I like being in a tucked-away corner like this, where the sun has limited access—

as if its playground were no more than some tree-top or black cliff face. If I find a corner of a hotel room where I can get a sidelong glance of a bit of the sea, I'll sit there for a good hour, with Petra laughing at the fact that ever-active Martin (she's kind enough to avoid the fashionable word 'hyperactive') is sitting down.

There is still some magnolia blossom in my corner of the garden, adorning the earth with an ever-thickening carpet of pale-pink petals. It's just like the day when Martin brought me the sensational news of what amounted to a miracle, and I reacted like a complete idiot, needing to come out to this bench to recover from my own bewilderment. I ran slap into a patient with an IV drip stand, and he was smoking, so that I all but set fire to my white coat, as well as nearly breaking his leg.

And here I sit, yes, here you sit, Martin Montag, and the spring has acquired a definite end-of-season feel, as on a certain day on this same bench three years ago, when you'd been behaving like a fool towards Martin, your favourite patient, in a shame-induced state of shock, while bowled over by your first sight of Jadwiga. And this is spring at its height, with not long to go before it makes way for summer, like a girl only in name who's on her way to becoming a mature woman.

The shortness of breath is still there, and the pain in my upper arm has increased its nagging. But I yield to it. I'm resigned to this discomfort, whatever its cause. I'm resigned to being on this very bench if something's going to happen to me, resigned to being out in the open air, and I even wonder if I could be bothered to call for help if what I call DP, the Dreaded Pain, should afflict me.

It's some time since I heard from my friend Martin Martinetti and it would of course be nice for me and for both of us if I were to give him a ring before my heart gives up on me, if that's what it's going to do.

He answers at once, and pure joy surges through me, as always, when I hear my one true friend's lyrical tenor and that French German of his, fleshed out with unadulterated French, altogether true to form: we haven't spoken for a minute before he's made me laugh. I feel a twinge in my heart as I laugh and continue to view myself from without, as if I were one of my patients.

I let Martin prattle on while I wonder what excuse I can find to cut him short if DP should strike while we're talking.

He's just finished his exams, which went well: from this summer on he'll be better paid for his plumbing. Jadwiga's in the thick of exam preparation, with only two years to go before she gets her permit. When she's finished her exams they're going on holiday to Kolberg. It's a short drive to this Baltic paradise, they'll be in the bosom of her large family, and Martin now speaks such excellent Polish that he's showered with praise from all sides, and it's such a relief, he says, to leave one's native language behind. Come on,

Martin, isn't French the finest language in the world? You could say that, he says, but it's a healthy thing to change from one mother tongue to another. (A thought which I'm in no state to follow up on, with my heart the way it is.) And such people! Jadwiga's family are wonderful, wonderful, *des gens extraordinaires, tellement spirituelles*: our western culture simply can't produce people like that: their souls are Slavic souls, on an unbelievably higher plane than ours. And their cooking, *mamma mia!* Their stews and their sour cream! And cakes of such quality that they're flown to Queen Elizabeth of England from the *Konditorei* in Warsaw, the cake shop, my friend, where Jadwiga's aunt worked before retiring to the delightful town on the Baltic where she now puts her culinary skills at the service of the family. As for the birthday cake for little Jadwiga's second birthday, he's never seen nor tasted one like it, and don't the French say that nothing in the baking line surprises them? What about *Babette's Feast?* I say, and Martin says oh yes, Babette, but Aunt Krystyna, too, is divinely gifted in the art of cake-making, and the difference between her and Babette is that she bakes for gourmets with such high standards that it takes at least seven generations to develop taste buds like those of Jadwiga's family. Whereas Babette's artistry expended itself on dimwits with the dullest of taste buds—which has a certain charm, it's true, a certain charm. And I listen with pleasure to my dear friend Martin's repetitions—they're a little like politicians' repetitions—while

I continue to wonder what sort of family he's really from, this mysterious friend of mine who's so eloquent on every topic under the sun apart from himself at the pre-down-and-out stage. I teased him once about how he was surely a down-and-out by birth, and he looked at me as if inspired and said: 'You've hit the nail on the head! A born down-and-out! You're talking to him!'

And now he's intent on coming to see me, and what would suit me best for that is first thing tomorrow, Friday, at my place: I'll be whiling away the time, I say, Petra will be on duty, we'll have a talk, just the two of us, I say, and Martin laughs, assuring me that he had not thought of bringing little Jadwiga to see such a champion child-frightener as myself. I reply that I'm not a child-frightener, as the evidence shows: children do unfortunately notice me when they run up against me, but that must be because I act as if I haven't noticed them. I'm not a child-frightener but someone who's frightened of children, and I remind him that I've had this diagnosed medically, with documentation to prove it. Dr Martin Montag, certified paedophobe! Martin laughs again and I join in with my own laughter as the twinge stabs again, worse this time.

Martin asks if I'm tired and I say yes, I am tired, as it happens, and he says he can hear it in my voice and he impresses upon me the need not to drive myself so hard: I have far too long a working day, he says, and must get out of the habit of going to the hospital on Saturdays. I tell him that all I'm doing is looking in, but he says it's unhealthy to work like that. And I know it's unhealthy but I'm still not going to change: I'll maintain my unhealthy working habits to the very end. So I keep silent.

One can never teach one's friends anything, says Martin, except by example, or by mentioning something to them *en passant* while barbecuing, there's no other way. And I say I'm one of those unfortunates who don't barbecue, as he knows, so that not even that approach is open to me: there's no way at all that I can influence friends of mine. Martin then says I'm fortunate in my surname, how well it suits me. No-one but a Montag—German for Monday— could talk the way I do.

I know; I might as well be called Martin Hangover, the first thing that people think of when they talk to Montag, the Monday man. Fate even took the final, decisive step, seeing to it that it was on a Monday that I came into the world.

'In your literal-minded Germany people have names that suit them', says Martin Martinetti.

'Does that mean that in your abstract-minded country names like Martinetti are purely a matter of chance?'

'That's the name I chose for myself. And it's not French, I'm glad to say.'

'You chose it yourself? Isn't Martinetti your family name?'

'No.'

'Oh? Where does it come from, then?'

'From an aunt in Antibes. She married a man of Swiss descent: it was his name.'

'What's your original surname, then?'

'I can't remember.'

'May I ask you why you changed your name?'

'No, you may not.'

'I know literally nothing about you from before you became a down-and-out.'

'So we're quits. I know nothing about you before you enrolled in the Medical Faculty.'

'Listen, my dear,' I say (yes, we call each other 'my dear'), 'I don't have time now for this talk of the past.'

'Me neither. It's always best to look forward, that's the important thing, and especially when walking on foot from Paris to Berlin.'

'That was really something! To even think of doing such a thing! Let alone bring it off!'

'You're right. But it didn't do me any harm, you know, all that walking in the past, when you look at how I am today.'

'Let's be thankful for that, my dear. It'll be good to see you tomorrow.'

We say goodbye, one friend to another, and I add aloud when I'm certain we've both rung off: 'That's if I'm not dead and gone.'

YES INDEED: IF I'm not dead.

That phrase never passed Martin's lips. He behaved always as if death could not touch him, even during those three days and nights of intensive care when I feared he wouldn't stay the course. I was losing sleep over a patient, something I don't normally allow to happen; if I did, there'd be no point in continuing in the job.

It was only during our first conversation that Martin showed the slightest recognition that he was a mortal being, or any sign that it mattered to him if he was.

HE WAS IN such a bad way that he looked as if he were fifty, even though he was only thirty-one. Like me; born in the same month, too: April (the cruellest month, as the poem has it): dirty, but not foul-smelling; black under the nails; and with clothes hardly of the cleanest. Yet behind the down-and-out you could sense the man of quality. The man of intellect as well: his swift flight of thought, his sparkling humour.

I changed tack, quick as anything, when I realised I had a complex case, a star of a patient, on my hands, and a Frenchman at that. I have to admit I'm a bit of a snob where anything French is concerned. So why not a French patient, even if he is a down-and-out?

'It'll have to be a combined effort if you're going to get

through this,' I muttered, to give myself time to think afresh about how to handle the case.

'Who says I want to get through it?'

'None of that whining, thanks. We're going to have to work on this together, with no holds barred, if we're going to kill this tumour. If you have any doubts about that I'm not coming anywhere near you.'

The patient looked at me, amazed, and said: 'It's the hero Siegfried reborn!'

'Who? What?'

'Siegfried the Dragon-Slayer. You're Siegfried the Tumour-Toppler.'

I laughed and said there'd be time for leg-pulling later on. 'So what's it going to be?' I asked.

'It'll be as you say. For the moment.'

'And your mind says so? Not just your mouth?'

'I'll see to it that it does. But the mind is its own place, remember: it'll need to look before it leaps.'

The mind is its own place! Was this an impromptu poet on the other side of my desk, or was he off-loading a quotation on me? If it was Shakespeare I didn't recognise it. It must be Dante.

'We'll start you off on four or five days in the detox clinic. You'll be given withdrawal medication and you'll have to stop smoking as soon as you can.' (His notes say he smokes four packets a day, if he has the money for it. Four packets, eighty cigarettes, how in God's name is it possible? There are only twenty-four hours in a day! Does the man smoke in his sleep?)

'By the time you come out we'll have found accommodation for you, and we'll need to get you into the system double quick. You'll have the help of a counsellor from the psychiatric ward and I'll be happy to put in you in touch with charity workers from the church. May I do that?'

'I'm not religious.'

'Let's not split hairs. Are you or are you not going to accept this help?'

'Alright then. What chances have I of surviving?'

'I could answer that more easily if you were in something like the normal condition for your age. But we're dealing with chain-smoking here, and your liver has started deteriorating.'

A doctor, or at least this one, always tries to avoid a tone of outright accusation with a patient. I get angry if I hear of colleagues taking that line. I allowed myself to tear a strip off one such quack who said to a patient of ours, an old gentleman: 'You'd find the medicine easier to take if you hadn't drunk so much!'

What I try to do is get the message across indirectly, by avoiding the second person in talking to a patient about his smoking, even if it's clear he's been committing suicide by cigarette over an extended period, as this one had. And for goodness' sake, bio-freaks get cancer, as do teetotallers and other self-deniers! You could say self-denial is a kind of attempt at suicide. Not to mention boredom, of which much the same could be said.

The patient raises his hand in the manner of an orator, and says: 'If your liver is playing up, punish it!'

'I've not heard that one before.'

'I saw it hanging up in an Irish pub in Paris. But tell me, what would be the chances for a man of thirty-one in normal condition?'

'They'd be pretty good.'

'A seventy per cent chance of surviving? More? Less?'

'It's no use playing around with percentages. A patient has either a hundred per cent chance of living or a hundred per cent chance of dying.'

He laughed, only to have a pitiable fit of coughing. I mustn't forget to prescribe a decongestant for him.

'And we're going to do our utmost to see to it that yours is a hundred per cent.'

'In other words, if I'm going to get through this,' he coughed, 'I've got to get myself into better shape.'

'I'll give you three weeks to do just that.'

'Well, it took me nine weeks to walk from Paris to Berlin. I'll think of my rehabilitation course as if it were a third of that journey. I'll have got to Belgium by the time I've finished the course.'

'Sound scheme,' I say, by way of saying something.

'How tough is this treatment going to be?'

'For testicular cancer the treatment is always tough:

there's no way of avoiding surgery. And it's tough from the psychological angle too. You'll be infertile.'

'That in itself will be an advantage. Even if I were a conventional citizen I would never have children. Never.'

He could see my startled, tongue-tied reaction. He looked at me in such a way that I couldn't return his gaze. I stood up and eased the window open.

Before I could sit down again he asked: 'Impotent as well?'

'Let's hope not.'

'That's right, no point in worrying: I might well be dead before I find out.'

'If I have anything to do with it you'll win through.' (The doctor's tone is brusque here, there's no denying it.)

He gave a spluttering, bronchial laugh, and I sensed, to my relief, that he was reasonably well-disposed towards me.

'And what's the procedure for getting me into shape for this treatment?'

'We'll start with the detox clinic. I'll do what I can to get you admitted this week. Physical exercise is a key factor, no less than an hour a day, in whatever form you like, whether it's going for walks, gym, or cycling. And you must force yourself to do it, whenever you possibly can, while the treatment's in progress.'

'I normally walk for much more than an hour a day. The life of a vagrant doesn't offer much scope for lying around doing nothing. We need to be on our feet to find food and shelter, and to survive, just like wild animals.'

'That's never occurred to me,' I said.

'With my muscles and bones I could brave the heights of the Matterhorn; they're as sturdy as anything. It's my lungs that would let me down. On level ground I'm just great, as you can see. I walked from Paris to Berlin in nine weeks without even feeling I had feet. I was wearing good shoes, of course, proper walking shoes. One has to do things properly. There's no point in charging off on a trek like that in bad shoes: that way you'll soon have no stamina left and maybe an ingrowing toenail. Not to be recommended.'

'You must tell me about this. All the details. Sometime when we can have a chance to talk properly. Look, can you come and see me at my home, tomorrow? At half-past six? We could have a proper talk then; here at the hospital one doesn't get a moment's peace.'

This new patient of mine seemed to think it quite natural that his doctor should invite him to visit him. But it seems there's a hitch.

'Sorry. Can't do it. Not then,' he said. 'I'll be plastered by then.'

'But you're supposed to be drying out.'

'That'll start when it starts, and not before. People at my end of the social scale take one day at a time and one thing at a time. If we didn't we wouldn't survive for even a week.'

'Alright then. So where can I pick you up? Could we make it about half-past five?'

SO I PICKED him up as agreed and took him back to my place. He was so drunk that I thought it best to hold on to him (a broken leg would hardly have helped his treatment), but he was clear in the head and certain of remembering tomorrow what passed between us today.

I had even thought of giving him something to eat, but when it came to it I couldn't face having him hanging around. I find drunks tedious, even when they're not talking nonsense, which this one wasn't. Seeing them functioning in slow motion, with elbows falling off the edge of the table, and spilling cigarette ash on the floor, is more than enough to have to tolerate. And those repetitious mumblings, for God's sake! For someone like me, who's had to keep a rein on his impatience like a lion-tamer with the wildest of beasts, this is simply not on. I quietly thanked God that I'd mostly been spared the company of alcoholics in my life to date, as I have better things to do with that patience of mine, so dearly bought and carefully cultivated, than to squander it on dipsomaniacs.

Without preamble I took hold of my green overnight bag, opened it, and told him that I had put in it all the things needed by someone going on a short journey, plus two books about cancer for the layman, full of practical advice on diet, relaxation, exercise and so on.

Martin looked in astonishment at what was in the bag: shaving gear, toothbrush, shirt, dressing-gown…

'And I'll drive you to the hotel a bit later, it's right next to the hospital. You can spruce yourself up there so you'll look alright when you go into rehab tomorrow. They're expecting you at nine o'clock.'

'That's impossible; can't make it before ten. I'm as good as dead until nine at the earliest.'

'Alright then, but not a second later than ten. I'll come and look in on you tomorrow evening, on my way home.'

Martin peered into the bag, took out the folded dressing-gown, sat hunched over the bag with the dressing-gown in his hands and wept, bespattering with his tears the black underpants that I'd found in my wardrobe and never used.

'The sum of human kindness is contained in this bag,' he said, pointing to the pants.

'I never thought you'd get sentimental with drink,' I said.

'Nor did I,' he replied, and blew his nose. 'Why are you doing this?'

'It's the competitive spirit. I want to win this battle.'

'It's single combat, then, between you and the man with the scythe. I'm just on the sidelines.'

'That's not quite true. I'm set on destroying an enemy in the form of a tumour. And the enemy's in you.'

'I think you'd better drive me to this hotel. This Hippocratic theorising just before the blow falls is a bit hard to take.'

Yet he did confide in me, once we were in the car, that he was almost certainly in love with one of the gatekeepers at the zoo. The first thing he was going to do when he was finished with the detox treatment was to tell the gatekeeper how he felt.

A gatekeeper! That was a turn-up for the books!

It's true that he had told me with memorable emphasis that he would never have children, even if he were a respectable citizen. There was surely a conclusion to be drawn from that. Except that there was nothing the least bit camp about him. Oh well, some people show their colours and some don't.

I wondered how it could have happened that the system failed to pick up this patient's sexual orientation. It was an unfortunate oversight, too, as he hadn't been screened for AIDS, and if by any unhappy chance he was positive my struggle with the man with the scythe would be much less certain of success.

I WENT TO pick up Petra once I had got Martin into the hotel. She noticed that someone had been smoking in the car so I could hardly avoid telling her all about the man who had just got out of it.

Petra's jaw dropped for a moment. Then she said:

'There are clearly quite a few things I still don't know about you.'

'That's as it should be,' I said. 'That's how it always will be.'

'I'd never have thought you'd take your acts of charity as far as this. What you're doing is not the least bit professional.'

'There's imagination as well as professionalism, and the two should go hand in hand. And it is professional to do one's utmost to ensure that a patient survives.'

'If you were to apply that rule to all your patients you'd be paying them home visits and cooking macrobiotic food for them.'

'I know, Petra, it's never a simple matter knowing how far to go. But the doctor who thinks that a young French down-and-out and an old Bavarian pensioner are the same kind of case is deluding himself.'

'The fact remains' said Petra, 'that there's some kind of rapport between you and this Martin, or whatever his name is. You could easily have had another French down-and-out on your hands without giving him any kind of special treatment.'

'You're forgetting my snobbery about all things French.'

'I'm most certainly not forgetting it.'

'You may be right if you're thinking in terms of the strictest rules of play, but that doesn't mean that what I'm doing is wrong. One follows one's nose in this job; otherwise there's no point in doing it.'

'I only hope there's not another Effie on the horizon.'

'I know, Petra, I know. I'm not ignoring that.'

'I never want to hear of anything like the Effie business

again. I thought I was going to lose you.'

'I'm taking care, I'm taking care. But Martin's case requires special handling.'

'If I didn't know any better I'd think you were in love with him.'

'Then it would be unrequited love. He's in love with one of the gatekeepers at the zoo. Mind you, his spoken German is pretty odd. Maybe it isn't a gatekeeper. Or even a man. But there's no doubt about the zoo.'

'Can't you get the gatekeeper to deal with him, then? If it is a gatekeeper? With his spiritual welfare, I mean?'

'I'm not a spiritual counsellor. All I'm doing is giving him what most people would regard as practical help: supplying their basic needs: a toothbrush if a toothbrush is needed, or a dressing-gown, if that's what's required.'

'You can be unbelievably square at times.'

'Can you say that a doctor who drives his patient to a hotel and pays for his overnight accommodation is square?'

'You may not be square as a doctor but as a man you're dreadfully so.'

'Alright then, Petra; round off my corners,' I said, turning to look at her. We were home and just about to park.

And Petra clearly knew what I meant and began the process in the car.

IT WAS HALF-past six by the time I got to the detox clinic.
There was nothing special to report on the patient's first
day: he had taken his drugs, eaten reasonably well, and
slept for most of the day.

Martin was pushing a tray away from him when I
entered the ward. This was just like a film: a hospital drama
with the young hero wearing my pyjamas.

'You look younger,' I said.

'It's these wonderful beds,' he said, 'at the hotel as well
as the hospital. The real disadvantage of being a tramp is
that you never sleep in a proper bed. Still, if you can find
a nice barn to settle down in, that's a real midsummer
night's dream, especially when a German farmer's daughter climbs into the hay to keep you warm. Not that that was
necessary. It was too hot in the hay anyway, even before
she added to it. A midsummer night's dream, no less. And
I had come all the way to Berlin, too: on foot. On foot from
Paris to Berlin. Beat that!'

So my dear gay friend is all of a sudden sleeping in a
barn with a German farmer's daughter. So he could be bisexual. I'd have to ask him about that directly. What a pros-
pect! Like catching a man with his pants down. All I said
for the moment was:

'Should I check on your dosage?'

'For heaven's sake don't. I think I'm turning into an
angel before my time. I simply glide off on these doses. Just
watch.'

Then he jumped out of bed, though 'jumped' is hardly the right word, and circled round the ward's spacious, two-bedded bay with a walk that could only be described as a glide.

'You should find out what they're giving me,' said Martin, 'and take some home with you. It's pure moonshine. Who needs aquavit when you can be on this stuff?'

'You'd better enjoy it while you can. You won't get anything like that at our place.'

'I somehow suspected the good Samaritan would be short on goodness, except when it suited him.'

'You've got the Samaritan down to a T. How are you feeling?'

'Just fine.'

'No withdrawal symptoms?'

'Some sweating and some diarrhoea. Otherwise nothing. Those gliding pills make drink seem like weasel's water. As the English saying goes: Why drink and drive when you can smoke and fly?'

'Well, I hope the detoxification is always as painless as this.'

'No question of it. I'll be sleeping the sleep of the just while I'm in detox, forgetting that I'm not allowed to drink, and just watching television. I can't deny that one thing apart from a bed that I've missed while living as a tramp is television. I like those films about animals.'

'Do you indeed? So do I.'

'We could both go to the zoo when I'm better,' said Martin. 'You could meet Jadwiga.'

'Which cage is she in?'

'Hold on now, this is the gatekeeper I was telling you about. She sometimes lets me in for free. How about that for a privilege? To the finest zoo in the world!'

'You obviously haven't been to the one in Vienna.'

'I admire it at a distance. I'd have gone there long ago if I'd had time. But don't let's get sidetracked. You get most kinds of animals in the Berlin zoo, and the zoo park, for a city zoo, is the biggest in the world.'

'That's the best thing about being brought up in Berlin: the zoo.'

'I can well believe it. The zoo's made a tremendous difference to the quality of my life, especially in the winters. I would have been quite prepared to uproot myself from Paris and move here, just for the zoo, if I'd realised in advance what a wonderful place it is. It's nice and warm in the monkey house, and I'm a model of good behaviour there, making sure nobody notices me drinking, and the reptile house is ideal for having a quick one on the sly.'

I was gradually getting the message that Martin's gatekeeper wasn't a man, and mentally wiped the sweat from my brow as it became clear that this patient of mine was hardly an AIDS candidate; and what was more, that I, the doctor, had been spared the embarrassing task of quizzing him as to whether he was gay or bisexual. I laughed like an idiot with relief, while he, the patient in question, reacted with noticeable suspicion, clearly uncertain about what was so funny.

'I didn't know the gatekeepers in Berlin were so susceptible,' I said, and tried to smother my next burst of laughter with a superfluous cough and clearing of the throat.

'She's Polish, of course, and very possibly smitten with me. How can she not be if she smuggles me into the zoo and offers me tea from her thermos when the weather's cold?

'Well, she could be compulsively kind-hearted.'

'She's a woman of class: she plays the piano and speaks French. She's got a slightly crooked nose that makes her face really attractive. She looks like one of Wajda's leading actresses; dammit, what's her name?

'One of them's called Krystyna Janda: she's incredibly beautiful.'

'That's her! That's the one. She could be her twin sister. An identical twin.'

'This Polish woman could play a key role in your rehabilitation.'

'None of that practical talk, thanks. We're talking about a superior being who has fallen into my lap.'

'But surely this superior being has other things to do than rehabilitate you?'

'She's studying as well as doing her job.'

'And you're sure she doesn't have a partner?'

'There was no partner mentioned when I last heard. I asked her, just to make sure.'

'You're off to a good start, then.'

'I've got more than a soft spot for her. Yes, it must be serious, because I've even started learning a bit of Polish. But supplementary rehab, no thanks, not while you're on the warpath. I doubt if any patient could take that.'

'You should realise that this gatekeeper could be a very important factor in your recovery.'

He burst out laughing. 'You really are a man with a single obsession!'

'What do you mean by that?'

'You see everything in terms of healing.'

'That's what you should be doing, more than anything else.'

'I don't know if I can make myself matter that much.'

'None of that arrogance, please. You've got an entire hospital at your beck and call to see to it that you survive, a rheumatologist in Treptow dodging the system so that we could give you a place without insurance formalities, and me taking personal responsibility for you until you've got into the system.'

Martin gave me a cold look. 'I trust you're keeping a full record of what I'm costing you, toothbrush, underpants, and all?'

'You won't be able to pay me back if you don't live; remember that.'

'Don't be so sure of that. I have an aunt in Antibes who's pretty well off. She's never given up on me.'

'What sort of failing in her is that?'

'She knows her own people.'

'Do you mean your parents?'

I thought for a moment that my patient was going to hit me, and I was right: he raised his arm. But then he took hold with the other arm of the one he had raised to strike and said, with cold-blooded calm: 'If you're really concerned about me and my recovery you'll remove that couple from the agenda once and for all.'

THE LAST CLOUD has vanished from the sky, the pain in my heart is still there, and my face is still sweating. How beautiful the world is, magnolia trees and all, from my Late Romantic viewpoint! And still greater beauty awaits me: five layers of pink chestnut blossom, if I don't die first. At some stage this world and all that is within it will have to survive without me: today or perhaps even tomorrow, and all those patients with all their problems will have to live or die without the help of Siegfried the Tumour-Toppler. Including the self-pitying pensioner with the yo-yo tumour whom I've met before, I'm sure of it. What is it about him that's so familiar? His voice? His walk?

IN GENERAL I don't ring Petra from work, and I know she'll be surprised if I break the habit, but in case I'm doomed to die a sudden death I'm going to ring her anyway, so that I can hear her voice just one more time and hear her laugh once more: so that I'll have given myself the chance to hear her voice before my heart fails me altogether, if that's what it's going to do.

Petra answers with obvious pleasure and no hint of suspicion of anything strange about my phone call, but she's not sure that we should sit out on the chestnut terrace, because she's been chilling our favourite rosé wine and baking cheese puffs (it's a habit of ours to celebrate spring with rosé wine and to revive memories of our first evening at the Ankerklause Tavern), and the balcony's really lovely, she says, the black tulips are starting to open: shouldn't we sit there instead?

So I make a compromise suggestion which finds favour: that I'll ring her when I'm about to leave work and arrange to meet her at our Chestnut Club, where we'll have one drink contemplating its layer upon layer of blossom, and then we'll ease up to the balcony and the black tulips.

'But of course', she agrees, and I want to spend longer talking to her, but I'm afraid I won't be able to conceal from her any longer how I'm feeling physically, so I make as good a job as I can of saying goodbye to her ('See you shortly, darling Petra') in case there's never going to be an opportunity to improve on it.

DARLING PETRA: MY gift from heaven. I remind myself every day of what other husbands have to put up with: nagging, tyranny, tetchiness, fussiness. Whereas I have the disgraceful luxury of minimum interference in every aspect of my existence, and tetchiness is so foreign to Petra's nature that I feel at times there's something suspicious about it.

The more I get to know Petra the more I appreciate her uniqueness and how close she comes to being something of a complete human being: as close to that ideal as any human being can aspire, if what the books say is true; and how she emerged unscathed from the horror of her youth: the child of a mentally ill mother.

Never knowing from one minute to the next, or from one day to another, what her mother would get up to: whether she would be happy or sad when the children came home from school—laughing or howling—or whether she would cook something that day and if she did, whether she would perhaps cut up a rubber glove with which to decorate it. ('It's such a bright yellow colour!') Or put pepper in the glasses of water. ('Pepper's so good for you!')

And her little brother Tertius, with the name suggestive of some mental disorder: as much of an enigma as Petra herself. You couldn't ask for a more open, entertaining, good-natured person. Amusing, like his sister (and what comes in handier than humour for survival purposes?). The only thing wrong with Tertius is those two dreadful children of his: so much so that I don't encourage family get-togethers as such. That's not to Petra's liking, of course, but she doesn't rail at me about it: I find ways of making up for it, like organising at regular intervals an evening out for the four of us when the children have gone to bed. That way Petra and I can meet her family without the distractions becoming unbearable.

Petra tolerates my absurdities and eccentricities, probably because the more or less normal life she finds herself living has come to her as such a divine gift that she's grateful for every day that's passed since she broke free from the family plot in which she, her mother and little brother were buried—and especially grateful for the days and nights she's spent with her big, strong, excessively bright, relatively sane, fearsomely bearded Martin Montag. Who, like her, is fond of music, specifically of singing, just a few operas (yes, we're fond of the exactly the same operas, with no extras on either side!), and the Beatles. 'Love me do', that was the song! And like her too he's fond of seaside walks and bathing in the sea (within limits), and Istanbul is her fairytale city ever since Martin Montag introduced her to it.

And Petra's beloved Martin, up to his eyes in his work as a doctor, nevertheless finds time to do all he possibly can for his wife. He cooks twice a week, and always on Sundays. One or two evenings a week they go out to dinner, as far as Petra's working hours permit, and Petra cooks twice a week too, but Martin won't let her do any more in the

43

kitchen than he does. On Wednesdays they eat leftovers, or perhaps the notorious *Abendbrot*.

Martin has furthermore laid it down that a cleaning lady (a relative of the other Petra, the Turkish one, he won't have just anybody) should come once a week, as he won't let Petra clean out the bath or scrub the floor. Nor will he do it himself, even though he knows how to: he was brought up by a mother who made him and his sister do an equal share of the housework. Unusual, that, and progressive, to say the least, and he's most grateful to his mother for the fact that he can cope with household chores and do the cooking: roast potatoes in pork fat and onions, for instance, with a rosemary garnish.

Once a week at least, and most often on Fridays or Saturdays, we allow ourselves an evening out: whether for a concert, the cinema, or the theatre. Sometimes Martin and Jadwiga join us; and sometimes Petra's brother Tertius comes along, either on his own or with Jana. We're a hilarious crowd, all of us, and especially Jadwiga, and we have such fun and laugh so much that I suspect we're sometimes frowned upon in restaurants, and I love Jadwiga to bits and have no problem with that: it's enough for me, loving her as I do, that she should exist, with that delightful mouth and delightful laugh of hers; and it's such a relief to me that there's never any need for me to touch her, ever, even with my little finger, or for her to touch me. And I don't have the slightest feeling of guilt towards Petra, because I love her too, no less, but it's a different kind of love, and in my mind I call the two of them Jad and Pet (sometimes merging the two together, into Jape or JP). I would lie awake at night composing poetry about them if I had the talent for it, and that's what I do, in fact, even though the best I can come up with is sweet, long-drawn-out nothings just as I'm going off to sleep.

I buy for Petra all sorts of feminine finery which I know other men would have no idea how to choose. My sister Erna helped me with this in the early stages. But as time went on I developed the habit of getting help from the shop assistants: I would choose the ones that were best dressed and best made up. I buy dresses for my beloved Petra, nightdresses and jewellery, and even toiletries. I know what kind of lipstick suits her best. And Petra is proud of me and of the ways in which I manage to comply with her wishes, and boasts to her friends and to her sister-in-law of her beloved Martin. He's something altogether special, she says, he can buy dresses for her with his eyes shut, and Jadwiga has let it be known that in her view her own Martin, who can do anything and who knows everything, as befits the man of good taste he is, having been introduced at an early age to French fashion at the highest level, even he would not be able to compete in this with his namesake, and my friend Martin is such a good friend that he reacts without jealousy, simply looking at me with pride as Jadwiga shows off her most recent present from me—as if

I were a son of his who has just learnt some altogether incredible skill, in the face of all the evidence of what might be considered likely.

Yes, he looks at me with pride, this friend of mine. Even so, it's he who comes closest to seeing through me. What is it that makes Martin Montag pamper his wife? Would he make such a fuss of her if he didn't feel the constant need to make up to her for the fact that she's got herself stuck with half a man, instead of a whole one?

WHEN I FINALLY rise from the bench and shuffle off I'm dragging my feet behind me like a ghost. It must be my heart: climbing the stairs is such heavy going that I feel I'll hardly make it to the top. Why didn't I take the lift? Is there really any point in going to such pains to make life difficult for oneself?

Fortunately I do make it all the way back to my room, unassailed by colleagues, patients, or secretaries. The windows are now offering shade, and it's somewhat cooler in the room. I leave the white coat on the chair and put on my suede jacket. I then lock myself in, exactly as if I'm keeping interruption at bay while a patient undresses. Why am I doing that? I'm supposed to be leaving, but I can't bring the day to an end, and yet I can't stick it out here a moment longer. I've started shivering.

I'm just about to turn off the computer when I sit down for a moment, listlessly, on top of my white coat. This doctor's going to be walking around in a crumpled coat tomorrow, if he's going to be walking at all. If indeed there's going to be a tomorrow for this doctor, who was all set to throw professional standards to the wind and rush off home, but who now is fiddling with the computer instead, going over the tumours of the day as he usually does at the end of a working day: making a final check to see if he's overlooked anything, or if he can refine the plans for treatment. What we have here is a policeman, impassive as glacial ice, investigating the tumours with a view to exposing the most violent and lethal of psychopaths. He now focuses his x-ray eyes on the oesophageal tumour from which the second-last patient of the day, the soft-spoken, neatly turned out whimperer of the words: 'Why me?' was suffering. It's a round tumour and fiery red: you might think he had swallowed a yo-yo.

TUMOURS ARE MY personal enemies and I do all I can to keep up my strength and determination in battling against them. Every day, before I go to work, I toughen myself up like a true Spartan warrior. I go running. That's the way to acquire the stamina essential for fighting, whether it's a question of short, sharp assaults or prolonged warfare. Without stamina there's no hope of victory.

I get up in the mornings at half-past four. (On Saturdays I sleep till half-past six and on Sundays till half-past seven. I don't usually go running at weekends, though I'll occasionally do what I call my Sunday marathon if the temperature's right for it.) I drink one cup of Nespresso before I go.

My favourite route is along the Landwehrkanal, by the weeping willows and restaurant boats, over the Baerwald bridge, and past the Altes Zollhaus and Brachvogel restaurants. It's best when the canal is iced over. Then I sometimes go skating, with a half-drowsy swan for company. If there is such a thing as happiness, this is it: skimming the ice in circles, alone and in pitch-black darkness, with no living creature around save the swan. This, for me, is ecstasy. The ice cannot always be trusted, unfortunately. But this winter luck was on my side, bringing moments of bliss, morning after morning after morning, or rather night after night after night.

I'm back home by twenty to six. I take a shower by the glimmer of the light in the passage and scrub myself from top to toe with a long-handled brush. I get dressed in clothes that I've got ready the night before. My breakfast consists of muesli which I've left to soak before having the shower, yoghurt with honey, half an apple or half a banana, maybe a kiwi fruit, and a cup of coffee with hot milk. I glance through the paper while I'm eating.

At ten past six I go into the bedroom. I turn on the reading light on my side of the bed, sit down and look at Petra.

I look at her, my best beloved, never so beloved as now, when she's sleeping, and reflect upon this wondrous being, so dear to me, who is busy dreaming, and I ease myself in beside her, into the dream, and on rare occasions allow myself to touch her, ever so lightly, on the shoulder or the cheek, after first closing my eyes.

I then set off for the hospital, with my mind on the tumours of the day but also on Petra, imagining her turning on the radio, drinking the coffee I made for her, and having a shower. I'm at my desk by half-past six, thus starting the day's work with half an hour or an hour in hand, quite undisturbed. That's essential for my campaign of extermination.

I put on my white coat, drink a glass of water, sit down in front of the screen and subject the day's tumours to ruthless analysis, viewing them with ice-cold hatred. 'Hate' and 'heat' may sound much the same, but my hatred is cold and calculating, directed against an enemy intent on taking life: life that is in my care. I think up the best possible ways of exterminating those tumours, every single one of them: how I'm going to set about wrenching the life out of each one of them, as if it were afflicting me personally, while at the same time doing as little harm as possible to the suffering human being, my patient.

In my methodology the affliction and the patient are as far as possible separated the one from the other. I think of what the patient was like before being subjected to occupation by the enemy, and also of what the patient will be like when I've got rid of the unwanted invader.

It's important to ward off the patient's fear of the tumour. To make sure the patient takes a stand. To correct any errors the patient might make in speaking of this life-consuming parasite. To say to a patient who asks what he or she can do about a tumour: 'What you mean is: what can you do to FIGHT it?'

Tumours are not brainless idiots wandering aimlessly in herds. They are sharp and alert, with minds of their own, and have clever ways of standing their ground and resisting invasion and treatment. Each new case requires its own approach and a tailoring of the treatment to suit it: an awareness of how much radiation to use, and of precisely where to direct the rays and when to use them, the aim being to destroy the infected tissue with minimum damage to the healthy tissues close by. That, for me, is medical practice at its best and most admirable, and where the future lies— in finely adjusted, aesthetically tempered radiation, rather than in poisonous liquids or surgical curtailment.

I have to say, if I'm honest, that I'm against surgical treatment, unless it's of the ultra-modern kind, involving laser technology and only the most delicate of incisions. Traditional surgery is a slapdash and medieval form of treatment, which modern technology is rendering superfluous. Surgical treatment is not really treatment at all: it's just another way of disposing of rubbish. And on top of that I'm not, on the whole, over-keen on surgeons, those hearty, aggressive, barbers-cum-doctors who tend to cut off more than is necessary. And if it turns out that one of these latter-day barber surgeons is a pretty young girl, my system is thrown out of kilter altogether and I simply have to look the other way.

Patients are generally at a disadvantage in their dealings with surgeons, too often receiving bad advice and being encouraged to have operations which could be avoided. Such advice is given pushily, as if it's a virtue to 'get on with it'. A strange motto, this; mine would be to put off the operation until all other remedies have failed. I would never submit to the knife unless my life depended on it. I've seen so many cases of things going wrong: infections, blood clots, one complication after another. Haven't I just!

Radiotherapy is the neatest method I know of countering cancer: the one that harms the patient least. That's why I've learnt to make it my own. I rejoice in every case in which radiation alone can do the trick, and the patient is cured and relatively unscathed after treatment. I'll never be reconciled to the drastic remedies of latter-day alchemists and barber surgeons, and hope I live long enough to see the holders of such positions greatly reduced in number, while I and my ray gun, and its opportunities for hitting its intended target with absolute precision, go from strength to strength, destroying the murderer in the patient's body while sparing the body itself.

WORN OUT AFTER the day's work and worn out with the pain in my heart, I make an effort at gritting my teeth and concentrating on the oesophageal tumour in the 'Why me?' man, the neatly turned out patient who strode to the end of the corridor after moving at a snail's pace in my consulting room.

It's as if he's swallowed a teeny weeny yo-yo. A red yo-yo. A fiery-red yo-yo.

THERE'S NO MISTAKING IT. I WAS COMING HOME FROM SCHOOL.

I WAS ACTUALLY COMING HOME FROM SCHOOL.

There's a haze before my eyes. Isn't that what happens to people who are dying?

I quickly invent a method of checking whether I'm still here or have passed over: I put my index finger to my nostril. (Here's someone who knows how to act in a tight spot!). My finger-tip detects breathing. So Martin Montag is not dead yet.

He closes his eyes so that he won't know whether or not he's seeing just black. He tries to breathe slowly; counts up to a hundred and eighty.

When I reopen my eyes again I see the screen in a blur and the room too—has dusk fallen already?—and my heart's still acting up. So I'm in just the right place—in my own kingdom with the door locked—for not being found until after the pain has had its way with me.

But it's not my heart. It's the hands of the second-last patient of the day. Those hairy-backed hands which he raised to the crown of his head, those hairy paws, and the triangular birthmark on the index finger of his right hand.

He should have had that birthmark removed.

EVERYTHING IS NOW as it should be in my room and of course dusk has not fallen yet. I stand up like any other man in the prime of life and walk to the mirror. Mirror, mirror on the wall, says nothing wrong with your heart at all. There's no trace of pallor on your nose or of sweat on your forehead.

The patient's notes say he has a first name, but it's not what he said his name was. The surname's an unusual one, which I've seen before. Another patient's name, perhaps? Or a name from my school years?

And this man with the birthmark who has a name must surely also have somewhere to live.

Yes, fifteen to twenty minutes' walk from the park with the waterfall: perhaps he's lived there ever since I used to come home from school.

I was coming home from school.

I'M ALWAYS COMING HOME FROM SCHOOL.

I'm straying from the path in the fine weather; I want to go into the park and walk along by the waterfall, and perhaps be a bit naughty and take off my shoes and socks and dip my toes in the water.

Why me? Why am I the one to be coming home from school?

It was me; it was I who came home from school.

He should have had that birthmark removed. A shiny black birthmark like that can be lethal.

IT'S ICE-CHILLED rosé wine that awaits me, the wine of which Martin, with the inside knowledge of a French *bon viveur*, spoke so highly, as well as cheese puffs and the afternoon—of which there's now not much left—that was supposed to be the occasion for Petra and me to welcome in the spring, and now she'll be starting to expect me to ring and let her know what time I'll get to the Chestnut Club so that we can start our celebration.

But Petra dear, I can't come home now or go to the Chestnut Club, because I'm coming back from school when I was little and you have no idea of what that trek of mine from school is like—no-one has any idea of it—and today I need to go an awfully long way round to a certain address, and it may be such tough going that I won't even make it.

I lie to Petra that I can't unfortunately get away immediately. There's been a hitch. It's a high-risk patient—not one of mine—that a colleague has passed on to me while he's on holiday, and I have to wait around until the situation is clarified. She'll have to start our little spring celebration without me while the balcony still has the sun; and I'm dreadfully sorry. Petra asks if I'm getting a cold, my voice sounds so strange, and I may indeed be catching something: I have a heavy head and a funny taste in the mouth.

I look at it yet again and all around it, the yo-yo in the oesophagus of the second-last patient of the day, before shutting down the computer and realising that there's little hope of this toy, the yo-yo, killing him. There'll be an urgent question to answer after the weekend, if indeed the time left to me stretches that far, namely whether I should hand this patient over to a colleague or treat him myself. I could perhaps press for some leave while he's having radiotherapy so that I don't have to run into him, or even be aware that he's in the same building.

THE BACK STAIRS serve their purpose: I reach the car without being set upon by patients, colleagues, or secretaries, and there's a party atmosphere in the air, in the trees, and among the birds, and also, I hope, on the balcony at my place: a one-woman party, until I get home. That's to say if I get home. If the walk from school isn't so insuperably long and exacting that I get nowhere near to completing it, today or ever.

And if it turns out that I don't complete the walk I'll be left behind again at the underground station, as on the day when I was coming home from school, with no trains running any longer, either in this direction or the other, because time no longer exists; and because I'm outside and beyond what no longer exists it won't concern me any more that I'm betraying Petra, whose trust in me is total, or that I'm betraying my patients, whose trust in me is total, or that I'm betraying Martin Martinetti, my soul-mate and one-time priority patient.

If I were to think at all about my parents or Erna once I reached the station, it would only be with incurable misery and sorrow that they should have failed a little boy, once and for ever.

Once and for ever! Could I really do that to Petra? Petra, whom all men surely envy me having as a wife, and would envy me even more if they knew how she kisses, and how she smiles at me as I come close to her when the two of us are alone.

ONE THING WAS certain, and always had been: that I had no intention of tying myself down. Whenever I was questioned I said I was married to my job, with no room left for a mistress. That was true enough, but what I didn't say, and what was more to the point, was that I had no intention of having children. Not ever. So why get drawn or draw anyone else into a long-term relationship, with such a flimsy basis for it? The odd woman now and again would be better than nothing, though it might involve telling lies, and extricating oneself afterwards might sometimes be a problem.

But it was that spring evening by the canal that finally put paid to this bachelor policy, when the canal banks were crowded with people happily eating and drinking by the gleam of lanterns, and the lights were shining on the water, and even the dogs were taking it easy in the gentle twilight, when time, along with the sun, seemed to have sunk below the horizon. After an extended day at work I had come home on the underground, as my car had broken down. I was so exhausted that I was more than ready to take a restful seat among the spring revellers and watch the lights reflected in the water, or to lie down on the spot and wait to fall asleep; but I pressed on homewards.

Ankerklause was jam-packed: all the outdoor tables were occupied and there was a crowd of people standing out of doors. One of the girls among them had rosé wine in her glass. That struck a chord. I'm basically a red wine and beer man, but there's something about the approach of spring that makes me switch to rosé.

The rosé girl was laughing in low tones as I approached. Standing there in the light of a red lantern she made me think of the sorcerer's apprentice. The tilt of her head as she laughed made her sleek black hair leap like a living creature, sweeping downwards before coming snugly to rest by her long neck.

You'd have thought that kickers-against-the-pricks like me would be immune to hypnosis, but apparently not: this kicker went straight into Ankerklause as if beckoned there and allowed himself to wait, calm as a millpond, for the long time it took to get served. And I'm normally the most impatient of men. I asked, of course, for a glass of rosé.

I went back out and took up a position beside the girl with the low-toned laugh and the hair that came alive. Yes, it must have been hypnosis that brought me so close to her as it was eighteen hours since I had had a proper wash. I normally take a shower evening and morning and if I miss one I simply can't bear the smell of my own sweat.

I adopted a somewhat direct approach: there was certainly nothing apologetic about my stance at her side. It was rather that of an acquaintance wondering if there was a chance to have a chat. A boy in the group was clearly startled at my planting myself there as if there were nothing to stop me, but that was not my problem and the laughing girl with the hair was quite ready to talk to me.

Her name was Petra.

'That's a good start', I said. 'I had a friend called Petra when I was little; she had hair just like yours. She's Turkish.'

'Yes, that is a good start,' she repeated, giving her low laugh with the same tilt of the head, so that her hair came once more to life, nestling thickly now on the other side of her neck, like a cuddly cat's paw.

Petra and I raised our glasses and the boy in her group looked even more anxious.

It soon emerged that I was a doctor, dead tired and on my way home from being on call, and that it wasn't my usual practice to stop at a pub in such circumstances.

'But I saw you laugh,' I said.

'Did you indeed?' she said, and gave that low laugh of hers for a third time. I don't know if a poet would have called it an enchanting laugh, but I haven't found a better word for it.

I asked what she did and she was, of course, a nurse. She, too, was going home from work and wasn't in the habit of going to the pub after being on call either, but some kind friends of hers had lured her there.

'Won't they be disappointed if you desert them and talk to me?'

'There's no end to the disappointment of others,' said Petra.

'Where have you read that?'

'It's the story of my upbringing: the endless disappointment of others.'

'More than for the rest of us?'

'Perhaps.'

'How so?'

'My mother was a mental case.'

'That's a good preparation for marriage.'

'Indeed!' said Petra, so curtly that I was quite startled.

I've often wondered about that curt 'indeed!' of my wife's at our first meeting. And she went further: 'I'd rather be on my own than become a wife. At least as far as one can plan such things.'

'Then I'm in the same boat as you.'

'Strange. I half thought as much.'

'What about coming to visit me? Wouldn't that make a good second start?'

'It sounds safe enough to me.'

'I make no promises about that,' I said, and Petra came home with me. Just like that.

The first few minutes left no doubt as to what life would be like with the man she had met. He sat her down on the sofa and gave her red wine and nibbles. He then took a shower, after explaining his long lack of a wash in tones of such irritation that she started to laugh.

After the shower he came into the sitting-room in his dressing-gown and asked his guest if she would mind dreadfully if he lay down for half an hour. It was better not to be completely zonked when talking to a girl who bore his favourite name, he added.

She took no offence at that; not taking offence, indeed, is one of her specialities. When I came back after half an hour, fully dressed, she had fallen asleep on the sofa. I sat and watched her sleeping until she began to wake up. A two-hour vigil. Sitting quiet and inactive for that long was for me a personal record.

I gazed at that living head of black hair, which was now, like the rest of Petra, fast asleep. I played the game of looking into her eyes through her sleeping eyelids, through those shining, dark brown eyes, gazing into the oracular head of the woman to whom I cannot begin to match up and to whom I have learnt to entrust the capsule containing my life, the life-egg which she could smash in the twinkling of an eye.

I gazed at her for two hours and prayed to God (for the one and only time in my life) that I would be able to love her as a man, not as the robot I am, and knew that my prayers would not be heard, but I kept on at God all the same, in the certain knowledge that here and now I was living my happiest moments, that this was not just a leg-up towards happiness but was the high point of happiness itself, and I sat for two hours, blissfully happy, gazing at my sleeping wife (who I knew was my wife from the very moment that her hair turned into a cat's paw by her neck), and I loved her with my eyes, with all my heart, fresh from the shower as I was and mercifully not smelling, not for the time being.

She began to wake up and there was no disguising the fact that I had shed two tears. One from each eye. A tear of joy from one, a tear of sorrow from the other. My wife on the sofa, now awake, looked at me and was quick to see that my eyes gave something away, but she pretended not to notice. She's quick to see everything: that's one of her specialities. When appropriate, she pretends not to notice. That's another speciality.

Once my wife was fully awake and had watched me spreading slices of bread in my own special way with red pesto and basil, all set to eat them at the kitchen table, a fairytale began that will never be forgotten, and even a man with my limitations knows that the like of this is reserved only for the elect: the man in question remembers at regular intervals how blessed he is with the gift of the original fairytale and the continuing fairytale, even though his role in it is only that of a cripple in the wings.

I ENJOY DRIVING and like sitting at the wheel in my powerful new car, driving in a daze on a perilous quest: perilous indeed, it seems, as I've nearly grazed the side of a delivery van. The driver blasts away at his horn, gives me a dirty look and flicks me a v-sign. Martin says that Berlin drivers are crazy: their boorishness and violent temper makes the traffic in France look smooth-running by comparison. The one thought that Berlin drivers have is: never give way. Are drivers as godawful as this in the rest of Germany? Or is it just in Berlin? I reckon they're worst in Berlin. And Martin says, with a pucker of worry and concern, as if he's talking about a loved one who's ill, that in this respect the city is still showing signs of the east-west divide which have not yet disappeared. That, for me, is a conversation-stopper. What sort of French logic is it to claim that the division of Berlin into east and west has had such a bad effect on the traffic?

The car heads on through this, the best hour of a Berlin afternoon, when the working day is coming to an end, and there's a vast sea of people at tables on the pavements under the trees, with their snow-white spring blossom, or on unsheltered street corners; but I'm not looking for a roadside table. What I'm concerned with is an address: the address of the man who has swallowed the red yo-yo.

I MAKE MANY detours around that address. I drift past my personal churchyard. It's my churchyard now, my memorial park. Never again in my life will I go into a park with a waterfall, I'll never again enter any ordinary park. Those are just ugly, bad parks, with live people in them. Now I stop by the crosses, by the dead people, my friends. With luck there'll be no yo-yo man where they are, where I'll soon be joining them, because he'll be going to hell along with the cannibals and pirates. And Mikki, who beat me into heaven when he drowned in the canal because those nasty people on the east side wouldn't save him, he knows everything: he knows where to find seesaws, puppet theatres, organ-grinders, ice cream parlours and ice rinks, and the amazing thing is that up there you can skate in the middle of summer! Up there you can do anything.

In my churchyard I found a new mother and a new father. They're my father and mother in heaven: their names are Sommer and Luft and they now live together side by side, though each of them was single in this world and they never even had children; so they'll be all smiles when I arrive and there'll sometimes be roast goose without its being a special occasion or even a Sunday, and Mummy Sommer will bake the best chocolate cake in the whole of heaven, and she's so kind, this Mummy of mine, that I'll be allowed to have three slices, and when I tell her about the nasty man with the yo-yo she'll take me in her arms and cry her eyes out and I'll comfort her, saying: 'We can't do anything about it, MumSomm, it's over and done with, and he's going to hell, where he belongs,' and she'll stroke my cheek and wipe away my tears and say between clenched teeth: 'To hell, where he belongs.' And MumSomm won't turn away from me, no, I'll be allowed a fourth piece of cake before I go to bed because I'm so dreadfully, terribly miserable, and she'll tuck me in under a massive duvet with a white cover, so incredibly white that it's whiter than snow is when it's freshly fallen and not a soul has trampled on it: not a human being, not a dog, not even one of those wretched crows or cats.

SOMETIMES WHEN I drop in on MumSomm and Daddy-Luft in the churchyard it's as though I haven't quite reached them. Sometimes I'm still on the way.

'Can't you get to us a little more quickly?' says Mum-Somm on such occasions. 'We're so dreadfully in need of a child.'

'Yes, and I'm so alone and in need too,' I say, 'and I miss Mikki. I'd like to get there as soon as I can. But how can I possibly reach you? I've no money for the fare.'

'You don't exactly have to pay to get here.'

'Maybe I could come over on skates when the winter comes.'

'That's one idea. You know the ropes, anyway.'

The ropes! Yes, of course I know them, of course I was only pretending, of course I'm old enough now to know the rollercoaster route to heaven and I sometimes sit out in the garage hugging the cord with which I'll make my ascent. I'm so light that I don't need my father's big rope, but if I leave it until I grow up the rope's what I'll need. The cord is just fine for a kid like me, the hook's already there in the ceiling, and I'll be talking to MumSomm and DaddyLuft as I climb onto the workshop table, put a wooden crate on the table, secure the cord in the hook with a monkey fist knot (scoutmaster Rainer's favourite knot) on the end, put the noose round my neck and say: 'I'm ready for the off! You've put the goose in the oven, haven't you, MumSomm? And it will be done by the time I reach you? It was roast goose you promised me, remember?'

I dangle my head in the noose and think it may not be so nice after all when I kick the crate away from under me and the noose tightens round my neck, but I know it'll only take a moment and I say, as scoutmaster Rainer often says: 'There's nothing to it, old chap.'

There's nothing to it, old chap, I repeat to myself. So I say goodbye to MumSomm and DaddyLuft, telling them I'll come next time, and Mums, as I also call her sometimes, says she'll look forward to seeing me, she can wait too, and I'm not to worry about the goose even though it was in the oven and is far more than she and Dads can eat; they'll save the leftovers for tomorrow.

Fortunately they stay where they are, so I can rely on them being there even though I'm not doing the roller-coaster today. I free my head from the noose and the cord from the hook and jump down from the table, flapping my arms as I jump. Then I hug my cord with its monkey fist knot and put it away in a plastic box which I hide under a heap of old cloth.

I then go to my mother and say it's an awfully long time since we had roast goose; when's our next day for goose? That gives mother an excuse to roast a goose at the earliest opportunity, and when it arrives father says that having goose now is an extravagance, but mother offers several good reasons for it. It's her dead mother's birthday, for example: she'd have been seventy-two if she'd lived, and celebrating that is hardly overdoing it.

ONCE MY MOTHER, and my sister too, had let me down, and my father had become no better than a hairy-pawed slob, I left home, to the extent that such a thing is possible for an eight-year-old. I was canny enough to see the way things were going, and circumstances were on my side because mother needed to have an operation and would be in hospital for two weeks.

Erna, my sister, said she could look after me and father, but I wasn't having that: she cooked such terrible food, I said, that I was bound to starve. I myself spoke to Mikki's mother and father, asking if I could stay with them, as mother was going to be in hospital for two weeks and the only things my sister could cook were such dreadful slops that I would probably starve to death: two weeks, after all, was quite a long time! They roared with laughter. Adile got Ozur to speak to mother, as her own German wasn't good enough, asking if they could help me out, as I was so set on staying with them. It was arranged that I would go home from school with Mikki and have supper with them, but sleep at home, but on Sunday evenings I could eat with them, stay the night, and go to school with Mikki on Monday morning.

I was full of self-congratulation at having engineered such a good arrangement. Such a good one, when I think about it, that I'm not at all sure I'd be alive today if I hadn't found that haven of refuge with Mikki and his little sister Petra, their mother Adile, and Ozur, their father.

MIKKI'S HOME WAS a fairytale world: their apartment was full of bright colours, spicy smells, warmth and laughter. Adile and Ozur were always talking to the children, joking with them, stroking their hair, and did not leave me out: they said I had beautiful hair, something I was hearing for the first time.

There was a constant coming and going of visitors and babble of voices at Mikki's which to me was incomprehensible: at home it was only Elizabeth, the cleaning lady, who came round, as well as Aunt Ida and Robert on Sundays. Some of the women visitors wore veils, even when seated on the sofa, drinking apple tea. When I asked Adile about the veils she said, mysteriously, 'It's what they believe.' I then asked if she didn't believe in veils like the other ladies. To judge from Adile's laughter this was the funniest thing I've said in my life.

When I asked my mother and father about this belief in veils they adopted a pitying tone, talking about 'those poor things', for whom they used the word 'simple'. At the same time my misunderstanding that these poor things believed in veils was corrected: they believed in someone altogether different from our Jesus, in a man who wanted women to have veils. I became very interested in this other man, Mohammed, and started inquiring about him at Mikki's. That was when my parents started worrying about their son's mental health and inflicted the parish priest on me. This genial if somewhat sentimental fisher of men found himself talking to a boy who was already a hardened sceptic, asking questions about where Jesus came from, his relationship to the Virgin Mary and Joseph, and wanting a full rundown on the Holy Spirit ... to the point where the priest looked at the clock, pushed in my direction ten pictures of biblical scenes (in which the Holy Spirit seemed to have got into difficulties, appearing only in diluted, unidentifiable form), and urged me to come to church, if only on such occasions as Easter.

One evening soon afterwards I heard my parents saying in a whisper, quoting the priest: '*The boy's a hopeless case, he's such a Smart Aleck,*' and it gave me something of a lift to think that the priest should be talking about me, a perfectly healthy boy, as if I were suffering from some incurable condition known as Smart Allergy.

The food at Mikki's was just amazing. Everything tasted good, though some of it was strange, and the smell was extraordinary, reminding me of incense and flowers and other things you can't eat. His mother spent many hours cooking. The vegetables and salad were usually chopped into small pieces. Ozur also made some of the dishes, such as yoghourt sauces or hummus.

I learned what the dishes were called in Turkish, and also the words for vegetables and fruit which I didn't know the German words for. We would sit for hours at the dinnertable, talking, talking, and laughing. They normally spoke Turkish at home, but now they spoke German because I was there. Adile spoke only broken German, so that I didn't always understand what she said: she sometimes had to say it in Turkish and Mikki or his father would translate for me. Little Petra was very good, too, at finding the German word for something in Turkish.

On one occasion at dinner they forgot this altogether and started talking their own language. I listened spellbound to this foreign music, and when they remembered that I was at the table they stopped in their tracks and Adile said: 'Apologies, Martin; we're not being polite to our guest,' and I said: 'I'm not so much of a guest that I don't want to learn your language.'

And they laughed with pleasure and Petra pointed to

every single thing on the table, telling me the Turkish word for it. After a few weeks I could understand a little and was soon babbling a few words. I sometimes spoke Turkish to Mikki and the other Turkish kids at school. I didn't mind the boys in my class teasing me and calling me Turkey or Mc-Turk: I just shook my heavy head—heavy with the hair that I refused to have cut until it became totally unmanageable.

One result of all this was that I was considered a godsend by the few Turkish grandmothers I had as patients, and who did not know German, because I could speak to them, more or less without an intermediary. And I was fortunate in that one of them had a son who owns a restaurant, where I, too, am welcomed as a long-lost son whenever I look in there. This excellent restaurant in fact played its part in getting Martin to build himself up in preparation for treatment. The grandmother who had been my patient, and who worked every so often in the kitchen of her son's restaurant, had got wind of Martin's predicament and would fuss around him denouncing German food in the most damning terms and shovelling wholesome Turkish food down his throat, maintaining that this or that spice would kill the cancer cells. I once went along too and had the pleasure of seeing my friend with them in a corner of the restaurant: my French vagabond transformed into a Turkish grandson. And Martin himself has explained to me at length that a vagabond needs to be able to transform himself into a whole range of other living creatures if he is to survive.

AFTER MIKKI HAD died by drowning—because those nasty people on the east side forbade the rescuing of children who fell in the canal—I continued to visit his parents and little Petra. Mother and father were not best pleased with my long sessions at their place, but pity carried the day. The poor things had, after all, lost their son; it would be a comfort to them, or at least better than nothing, to have his friend drop in from time to time. And there was also the fact that my mother and father knew their son well enough to know that it would have been hard to stop me.

Petra and I had no difficulty playing together for hours, even though she was so much younger than me and a girl at that. The strange thing was that I could stroke her hair, her long, glistening black hair, from the crown of her head to the shoulder; and I let her pat my cheek and hold my hand. Mikki's father, too, could put his hand on my shoulder without my recoiling in horror, and I also let Adile stroke my hair, which she said was the most distinctive and beautiful hair she had ever seen.

No-one else could come near me, however. I pushed mother away from me if she tried to stroke my cheek. This sometimes made her cry. But I was adamant and could not forget the day when I made this clear and burst into floods of tears, and she would not believe me, however much I cried.

When Petra and I got to play with Mikki's things she would sometimes start crying and say that Mikki couldn't play any more because he was dead. Then I would comfort her and say that we would meet, all three of us, in heaven, where all the dead people were good people, because the nasty old men with their yo-yos and the cannibals were in hell, along with Hitler and the pirates, where they belonged.

On one occasion when her brother's loss was making her weepy, I said to her: 'Why don't you call me Mikki? But don't tell anybody, whatever you do.' So I turned into Mikki, which meant that I had never once, on my way home from school, gone into a park where there was a long waterfall and a hairy-pawed man with a yo-yo: no, I was Mikki, who had died and drowned in the canal because I couldn't be rescued, and I had come to heaven, where it was so, so much better than down here on this wretched planet earth.

It was a good arrangement, Mikki taking up residence in me, and me in him; it meant that missing him came close to being less painful than it might otherwise have been. The metamorphosis was not complete, however, because it nagged at me that as long as I was Mikki himself I would never find a soul-mate. That was a word that I had found in a book somewhere, SOUL-MATE, and I knew for certain that that was what Mikki had been.

That was one thing that my tough little soul was right about. No-one took Mikki's place, not until Martin Martinetti arrived on the scene: a thirty-one year-old French

73

down-and-out with an affliction where it would truly afflict, and we became, yes, inseparable: to the extent that I
adopted the practice of systematically skiving off almost
every Saturday for half the time allotted to visiting Petra's
mother and eking out two hours or so with Martin, before
the weekend began in earnest for Petra and me.

MARTIN AND I met, as agreed, just before he was due to
start on his first course of chemotherapy. The place was
Brachvogel, the day was a day in April between our two
birthdays, and the smell of spring in the air was such that
it quite simply stank.

Petra had allowed me to sacrifice the part of Saturday I
normally shared with her after looking in at the hospital,
going swimming and visiting her mother. She regretted
every minute that we did not spend together, but this was
a worthy cause.

Well, it was and it wasn't. I really wanted to go home,
and I was just beginning to get irritated by this elaborate
mission of goodwill when Martin approached on foot and
my negative thoughts gave way to pure wonder. I'm not
sure that I would have known him if it hadn't been for his
curly head of hair. This man even moved differently from
the Martin I knew, and he certainly didn't look fifty, as he
had at his first consultation.

'*Bonjour,* my friend,' I said, 'if it still is you. Have you been in a time machine?'

'*Bonjour,* good day, to you too. Yes, this is a good day. I have indeed been in a time machine.'

'Where did you find it? I wouldn't mind some time travel myself.'

'But you've got your own time machine at home.'

'You're joking.'

'I mean Petra. She's your time machine. Mine was at the zoo.'

'I hope your problems haven't affected your brain.'

'I've come to the conclusion that Germans don't understand metaphors, especially when it's about love.'

'Well, I can't understand a word of what you're saying at the moment.'

'I'm saying that love is a time machine.'

'Don't forget that you've been drying out.'

'I'm not forgetting it. Maybe love is a kind of drying out, too.'

'I think we need to be sitting down to have this sort of conversation,' I said. 'I'm a bit worn out after swimming.'

'Swimming?'

'We go swimming every Saturday, five of us, in a lake not far from here.'

'But not in the winter?'

'Oh yes. That's the best time.'

'And do you take birch twigs?'

'No, we don't need them. It's bracing enough without them. Especially in winter.'

'How cold is the water?'

'It was nine degrees today.'

'This is Germanic insanity in the highest degree. I want to hear no more of it.'

'But you're going to. We go in twice, take a run between dips, and for the second dip we're naked, because our swimming costumes have got wet.'

'Stark naked?'

'You'd better believe it.'

'But what about passers-by?'

'Oh, it's off the beaten track. But we do get passers-by sometimes.'

'Good God! Five swimmers, stark naked, in a lake in a Germanic forest! And to think that this tribe has my health in its hands! What have I let myself in for?'

'You're in one of the best hospitals in Europe for successful treatment of cancer. The doctor in Treptow knew just what he was doing when he cooked the books to make sure you came to us.'

'That's what keeps happening to me: rescue in the grand style. Without me lifting so much as my little finger.'

'But you did lift your little finger. You stepped across the threshold in Treptow.'

'That's still the same old story. Give the devil your little finger and he'll take the whole hand.'

He then ordered a small beer. I wasn't happy with this special patient of mine drinking alcohol just after drying out, but he swore on his absolute honour that this was his fixed daily amount, and that he was sticking to it. He had bent the rules only to the extent of having a glass of red wine instead of the beer when he took Jadwiga out to dinner.

'Out to dinner?'

'Yes, I invited her out to dinner.'

'Who? '

'Jadwiga.'

'I'm not with you.'

'You know, the Polish girl at the zoo.'

'I don't believe it.'

'Me neither.'

'How did you manage to rustle up the money?'

'I've told you about that aunt of mine in Antibes. She likes giving me money, and sometimes I let her. This was one such occasion.'

'But how do you handle it? I don't imagine you've got a bank account.'

'There's Western Union, for one. Do you think me and my aunt are completely clueless about these things?'

'So it's Jadwiga that this love-talk is all about.'

'It's not about her: it's her. She's love itself, love incarnate.'

'Did you get an extra dose of those pills? '

'I don't need gliding pills. I glide with Jadwiga. Love is an exercise in gliding. In rising on faltering wings above the earth. Man's ancient dream of flying.'

'Congratulations! I'm very pleased for you. But I'm not sure I can take much more of this lyrical stuff.'

Martin was nothing daunted, however. After he had put away one of Berlin's best sausages with lashings of mustard (which was, of course, nothing like as good as French mustard, so why do you have so much of it? I asked) and some potato salad, and had gulped down his double espresso, he was full to bursting with the need to talk and came clean to me about that miraculous human being, Jadwiga.

The essence of it was that as soon as Martin was released from detox he went to meet Jadwiga at the gate of the zoo, spruced up, freshly shaven, and wearing a jacket and shirt borrowed from me. There was bright sunshine in town that day and when she had got over her astonishment at seeing this changed man, she agreed to go out to dinner with him in the evening. And at the restaurant things really took off. He told her about his illness, the detox, his weirdo of a doctor, and his life as a down-and-out, and she said she was in love with him, it was no more complicated than that: in love with him whether he was drunk or sober, in sickness or in health. He had then said: 'Even if I'm bald? ' And she had said yes, bald as well, and a tear came to her eye, because he had such beautiful hair, and what did he do then but depress her by saying that when his hair came back no-one knew what it would be like: he might be blond with straight hair, whereupon Jadwiga started weeping over the chop she was eating, as if that were the most dreadful thing that could possibly happen: Martin Martinetti blond, with straight hair!

But it was joy that won the day and astonishment at their having found each other, joy that it could really be true, that was the main thing, and the cancer was unimportant, a temporary setback that would simply have to run its course, and in any case Jadwiga came from a family of famous herbalists, people who knew of other remedies than just the traditional cures with drugs and radiation, and neither of them feared that the cancer would gain the upper hand, that wasn't even on the agenda: this man wasn't leaving this life, he was beginning a new life: that too was possible. And they laughed at this terrible cliché, 'a new life ', and Martin quoted a poem by Dadason in which the idea of a new life was mocked, while Jadwiga remembered one in Polish and translated it on the spot, so Martin decided to learn Polish and Jadwiga resolved to improve her French. She was an absolute linguistic genius, said Martin: he had never heard a foreigner speak better French than she did, and what a luxury it was to be able to talk to his beloved in his mother tongue and keep his dignity, instead of having to resort to obscenities in German with his appalling French accent. It was impossible to take seriously people who only spoke gibberish.

I had allowed myself to order a second small beer, because I was bound to listen to this account in detail, though I normally never drink more than one small beer before dinner in the evening, if that. And the screeching of the Brachvogel birds was enough to drive the customers in the beer garden, or me at least, out of their minds, so that I started getting drunk, and there was nothing for it but to order a third beer, another sausage with some more potato salad, and another espresso for Martin before proceeding full speed ahead on this terrible rollercoaster ride with him and Jadwiga.

We had been sitting at the Brachvogel for two hours and I had been listening to Martin's torrent of words for all that time, practically without interruption. His accent was so pronounced and his choice of words so wayward that I failed to take in half of what he was trying to say, and it was no better when he got on to their sex life. I'm still floundering in doubt about some of the things he said: about whether he was really telling me that Jadwiga had been good at finding ways of getting love-making to work with a man whose illness was giving him difficulties in an essential area, or whether I had misunderstood him as saying that for him the missionary position had been physically painful but everything had gone swimmingly when she was on top. Martin was not used to discussing sex in German and everything he said was in some way distorted. I would rather have forgotten this florid account altogether, for who wants to follow one's friends all the way into their bedrooms, even if they are one's patients, but this monologue with its grammatical errors and its tortuous construction of impossible variations on the theme of love-making is still painfully close to the surface of my consciousness, where it sometimes still surfaces, I'm sorry to say.

I felt sure that these descriptions of Jadwiga as an angel in woman's guise were exaggerated, that the man was in the confused and heightened state of mind of someone embarking on a new chapter in life in an unprecedented, contradictory way, with little capacity for holding everything together in his head and heart without going over the edge. But I had to eat those words, spoken to myself, when I met Jadwiga for the first time, and had to eat them again twice over when I first visited them. The amazing thing was that my brilliant friend's descriptions of the habits and home set-up of this woman were accurate. If anything he had not gone far enough.

What Martin was telling me, with the distracting screeching of the spring birds all around us, was that he had found an angel in human form, an angel with humour, an angel of love.

I interrupted him:

'Does she play the harp as well?'

'Let's not have any of that. She plays the piano, as I told you.'

'I'd forgotten.'

'How could you forget that she plays the piano? '

He was clearly hurt, as if I had said something unworthy of his angel in human form. There was nothing for it but to go quickly into reverse.

'I'm sorry. I have so much to keep in my head from one day to another.'

'Maybe, but I did tell you she played the piano.'

'True enough: you did tell me.'

'And she plays it damn well. Chopin, Eric Satie, the lot.'

But he was still hurt and humiliated, as if I had offended him on purpose, had actually tried to belittle his angel of a sweetheart out of pure malice. His mood didn't lighten until he came to mention Galvanistrasse, where Jadwiga had her nest.

'Just a moment, Galvanistrasse; is that within the city boundaries?'

'It's the coolest street in Berlin! That's typical of you city-dwellers, not knowing your own city! It's only vagrants and taxi-drivers who know it. Runners know it least of all. They just plod on in a haze of sweat without noticing the time of day or even where they're going.'

'I'm not that out of touch when I run. I do notice things around me. When there's enough light, that is. For half the year I run in the dark.'

'A night-runner? '

'I start the day with a run and the night lasts well into the day in Berlin.'

'Running in the dark! What kind of pervert does that? And you don't even know Galvanistrasse! I sometimes went there before I met Jadwiga. It's a wonderful place, where three waterways meet, and it's well off the beaten track.'

'Okay, okay. And what sort of a life does she lead, this Pole of yours?'

And he described her circumstances with such eloquence that an award-winning writer high on cocaine could not have done it better.

The plain facts of the matter were that she had taken over a penthouse apartment which she had got at a very cheap rent because it had so many drawbacks. You couldn't stand up properly in the bedroom except by the door ('but who needs to stand up to their full height in a bedroom?'), and the kitchen was no more than a cupboard (which did not matter, since Jadwiga had extended the kitchen into the passage, with a set of shelves, a collapsible table, and some folding chairs). On the other hand the sitting room was spacious and bright, and only part of it had a sloping ceiling. And there was a piano, a splendid piano, which was properly tuned.

And such an artist was this woman in matters of design and interior decoration that she had made everything in her sitting room into a harmonious whole. The mirrors and the plants gave such an effect of feng shui that you wanted nothing more than to sit on the sofa and lose yourself in meditation and nirvana, preferably without standing up again.

'Wouldn't that be taking relaxation a bit too far? '

But Martin left this little dig unanswered and pressed on without delay.

Jadwiga had shown him pictures of the apartment as it was when she first took it, and it was almost inconceivable that one woman could have transformed the place as she had done. Not without help, it's true: her brother had brought the parquet flooring from Poland, where he had got it at a low price. They helped each other to lay it, and then she had painted everything and made the shelves.

'So the angel is also a jack-of-all-trades.'

'I didn't know such people existed; though behind the Iron Curtain, of course, people have been thrown back so much on their own resources. This one can make something out of nothing.'

'Then she's one step ahead of Jesus himself: he needed water before he could turn it into wine.'

'It's no use talking to you! I'm describing to you a woman who is altogether incredible, whichever way you look at it. To think that I found her in a zoo! Can't you be pleased for me, man? '

'But pleased is exactly what I am! You've greatly increased your chances of pulling through.'

'As I always say, you think of nothing but this damn tumour! It's no use talking to you.'

'Listen: what am I supposed to think about if not this damn tumour? It's my job to see to it that it disappears. As if by magic.'

'Okay. Do you or do you not want to hear more about Jadwiga?'

'Haven't we just about covered it? Is there more to tell? Does she plan to work in the zoo permanently? '

'In her own way, yes. She wants to be a vet, and is going to evening classes in preparation for that. She should be able to start the full course in six months' time.'

'That'll be your most difficult time as far as the treatment goes.'

'What the hell difference does that make? She'll be there for me, however the treatment goes.'

'Do you plan to move in with her? '

'She wants me to. Her big worry is that I'll have problems with the stairs: there are a hundred and two steps,' Martin laughed.

'It's no laughing matter. You'll be so weak at the time that you're bound to find the stairs difficult, no matter how many steps there are.'

'This counting of steps by you and Jadwiga is ridiculous. It's killjoy stuff, pure and simple. Wouldn't a bit of encouragement be in order? Though I'm not sure that I ought to move in with her. What sort of fun will it be for her, starting a relationship with a poor wretch of a patient that she'll be nursing for nine months or longer?'

'My understanding was that the relationship has already started.'

'I think it would be much better for me to see this treatment out in the little room they've given me at the church.'

'Are you out of your mind?'

'I'm thinking about it.'

'Well, don't think about it. It's essential for you to have good care.'

'One can't be so damn practical in matters of love.'

'It's damned impractical to have cancer (let me remind you!) at the start of a love affair, especially your kind of cancer, quite apart from financial considerations and other small matters, so it's perhaps not such a bad idea to be correspondingly damn practical.'

Martin stared at me, his jaw falling.

'You Germans,' he said. 'They're right about you lot.'

'Don't you dare address me in the plural,' I said. 'Never again.'

'I went too far,' said Martin. 'Don't hold it against me.'

'Of course I won't,' I said, finishing my third beer, and because the whole situation had become so preposterous I went ahead without more ado and ordered a fourth.

'Do you normally drink like this during the day?' asked Martin, with an expression of some alarm.

'On this occasion, a special occasion, yes! It's not every day that a star patient of mine has just fallen in love.'

'I'm relieved to find you showing an interest in other

problems of mine than just the tumour.'

'I'm not in the habit of discussing emotional matters.'

'Your poor wife!' He urged this upon me in his own language, an occasional habit of his when making a point of special import: *'Ta pauvre femme!'*

'You may be right. But not for that reason. She and I can talk about anything. I meant that I wasn't in the habit of discussing emotional matters with people apart from her.'

Martin gave me a close look which I have never forgotten. What did he think of me? That I was sexless, a pervert, or a control freak? There is no doubt that something suddenly seemed to occur to him when I did not deny that there was some cause to feel pity for the woman who was my wife.

Martin Montag, who stood up with four small beers and two of Berlin's best sausages—potato salad, cucumber and all—inside him, was not altogether steady on his pins. When the passengers on a passing tourist boat started waving and shouting greetings he responded so effusively as to make the patient ashamed of his doctor.

THE YO-YO MAN's address is in a busy pedestrian street: a long unbroken line of tables and chairs with people strolling by, and chestnut trees which have blossomed so early that the papers and television are constantly commenting on it and showing pictures of them. It's not for any good reason that this has happened, of course: it's global warming. May hasn't even begun.

The front door of No. 31 is bright yellow, glistening in the sun. I look at the doorbells and sure enough, there he is, with the unusual surname, the first letters of his first name, and his profession: *Doctor: Head of Department.* I chuckle at this last bit because I'm here in a professional capacity myself, cool in the head but in hot pursuit of a devious debtor of long standing, my only business with him being to collect the unpaid debt, with interest and compound interest. The method of collecting it has yet to be decided.

I cross the street. The outer shell of the building is un-exceptionable. It's one of those ornate buildings from the turn of the century, in which the people on all floors are flower-freaks and taste-freaks, in the style of the second-last patient of the day, the clean-shaven pensioner with his pink silk tie.

A woman with straight, lustreless hair appears at a window on the first floor. She peers quickly in both directions before opening the window just a little. She hesitates again, then opens it all the way. She hastens to water some fiery-red flowers that are hanging down, stalk-length, from the window ledge, then looks down at the street as if there was something there that no-one could bear to see.

She closes the window quickly and disappears, a passing

scarecrow, a blemish on the building's perfect facade, with its smooth, varnished door.

I take a seat at the café opposite No. 31 and watch that bright yellow door, just in case the second-last patient of the day, or his wife, should risk coming out into the open.

I've had two espressos and have almost got through *Der Spiegel* when the front door of No. 31 opens and the second-last patient of the day does indeed come out, with two women in tow: the grey one who was with him at the hospital and the one who was watering the flowers on the first floor. She's looking right and left, left and right, as if she's expecting a fast-moving car in this street—a street closed to drivers.

The grey woman looks at the street as if the paving stones are going to rise up against her. But the second-last patient of the day saunters gaily ahead to the café next to mine, as if to say: 'It's me, ladies and gentlemen!', while the womenfolk follow like frightened refugees. If I hadn't seen them come out of the door of No. 31 it would not have occurred to me that the three of them were together, let alone from the same family, which they surely are: father, mother, and daughter.

A waiter rushes up and greets him like an obsequious servant. The head of the family responds in lordly fashion, clamping a companionable, hairy paw on the shoulder of the waiter, who points to the free tables, indicating that they can sit wherever they like. The head of the family walks with decisive steps to his chosen table, the women following at a distance. He stands by the table like a viking chieftain and gives a jerk of the head to each of the women, indicating that they should come and sit down. He sits down himself and they approach hesitantly, still at a distance, and then sit down looking furtively around them in case they haven't done the right thing: as if they're expecting some reproach.

But on this occasion at least the women do not seem to have been at fault because their host hands them the menus and is full of bonhomie. He even gives an unctuous smile as he takes his table-companions through the menu, and strokes his daughter on the shoulder while pointing out to her this or that choice of food. At the same time it's obvious from his behaviour that he belongs in other, grander company than this, but that for the present he can't do any better. So it's only fitting that he should be somewhat distant, as he clearly is, drumming with his fingers on the table and at intervals contemplating the view, as if he's going to give it a mark out of ten.

I watch the daughter as she looks through the menu. I know this woman, or have known her in the past. I look fixedly at her and know we have met, but I don't know where, or in what earlier life it could have been. Was it in one of the wards when I was a student?

The waiter comes to the table and is clearly asking the man how he is, for the man indicates his chest with a pat of his hand and shakes his head sadly, and the waiter in turn shakes his head sadly. Then the waiter is dismissed because they are not yet ready to order.

The mother and daughter are having some difficulty in deciding what to eat. They are all far from settled. The man starts reading selected parts of the menu aloud, as if the women were illiterate, blind, or foreigners. At last the younger woman seems to come to a decision, but the man shoots it down and offers his own opinion on what she should order. The daughter at once changes her mind and accepts his decision.

The waiter approaches with nimble promptitude as soon as they've put the menus down, and the man announces what they have chosen, loud and clear. I see him in my mind's eye in a court of law, passing sentence in accusing tones. And he wouldn't be content with passing sentence, no, he would put the boot in, leaving no doubt as to the faults and wretched character of the abject accused.

The food comes at record speed. The man moves cups and plates around on the table and rearranges knives and forks for all three of them, with surgical precision. Is he going to spoon-feed the women as well?

A friend approaches with a brief greeting and inquires after the man's health, and I hear a faint echo of his words this morning: *'Why me?'* The friend gives him a sympathetic look. Then the patient changes gear and starts talking to his friend with affection, and with the broadest of smiles.

Then the daughter's dead facial expression comes to life: she watches her father as if she's sizing up a stranger that she doesn't like the look of. She stands up and says, loud and clear: 'Please excuse me', and moves in the direction of the Ladies. The man sends his wife after her with a jerk of his head. The wife springs to her feet, suddenly acquiring swiftness of movement, and follows her daughter in an unscheduled visit to the loo, half-way through the coffee-drinking stage. Her husband, thus abandoned, remains seated at the table.

He's now talking to his friend in evident distress, in low, confidential tones. Then he shakes his head and says, raising his voice excessively: 'I've lost faith in psychiatrists altogether.'

All heads in the café turn at this declaration. The friend withdraws, taking his leave with some embarrassment. He walks off, the heads in the café return to their own concerns, and the man who has lost all faith in psychiatrists gives close attention to his slice of layer cake, heaped as it is with cream, and concentrates on finishing it. He drinks his coffee with finesse, settling his cup in its saucer after each sip.

A respectable man. Oh so respectable! As Martin and I would say, amusing ourselves, as we would, by looking at him from all angles with various observations.

The women return and sit down cautiously, as if they are unwelcome. The man looks sternly at them and seems to be criticising them. The woman is apologetic, but the daughter stands up and says, even more loudly than the first time: *'Please excuse me'*.

The man gives a threatening look and orders his daughter back to her seat, but she leaves with gestures of farewell in all directions, and continues to bid farewell, in the manner of Ophelia—*'Farewell, goodbye, adieu, auf Wiedersehen, auf Wiederschauen'*—all the way across the street, and disappears behind the smoothly varnished bright yellow front door of No. 31.

The man stands up quickly. The woman is too slow to follow suit: the man grabs her wrist and twists it. The woman does not bat an eyelid. He's in a hurry to pay the bill, and the waiter, who is not responding quickly enough, is now in his bad books.

And the window on the first floor of No. 31 opens, and the sun shines on the daughter's face as she glories in her triumph and cuts the red flowers from their stalks, throwing them onto the pavement with a smile. It's the remains of a lovely smile on what was once a beautiful face, the face of the girl that was, the human being that was.

The man crosses the street with brisk, military strides, shaking his fist at the window. The woman tries to hurry after him, but is limping. Does this mean that she's been kicked in the shin under the table? Or has she been limping all the time without my noticing it?

A young girl comes to clear the table, sees the two plates

with half-eaten pieces of cake, and looks up at the first-floor window. She shakes her head slowly. And the sun shines on the woman at the window who bursts into rusty laughter, like a rag doll that's capable of making just one noise.

I suddenly feel cold, as if there's been a complete solar eclipse, so I put on my suede jacket and button it up to my neck. That makes me no warmer, but the sun is still there, uneclipsed, its gleams very evident in the linden tree on the other side of the street, between buildings Nos. 31 and 33.

And that shadow of a woman with her rusty-sounding laugh, issuing as if from an empty cask, was not always a shadow, but was once a girl of flesh and blood, full of joy in her good moments, with long hair and a high ponytail. I called it a fountain, and she enjoyed that.

The details of the story are coming together with lightning speed in my head, in Martin Montag's marvellous memory. The medical report is there in his mind, an open book, readable from word to word and page to page. He still can't wait to get hold of it, however, to have it in his hands, and read it once more.

I COULDN'T POSSIBLY be mistaken: it's the girl with the auburn hair and the unusual surname. I didn't know much about her: she was in the ward for only a few days after I started there. But I spoke to her once and although I've never gone over it in my mind since then it's coming back to me now, with levels of tone and all, as clearly as if I were listening to a tape.

An eighteen-year-old girl who wanted to die, and die immediately. Who could not live. Who wished she had never been born. What are all the tumours in the world compared with the depths of her suffering?

But she was born, and she wasn't able to die once and for all, as she wished. She went on dying, week after week, month after month, year after year. How much longer can she go on dying: how many weeks, months, years?

I'm putting the medical report on this girl, the girl with the surname, in my briefcase. It's as though I'm watching a film in which I'm one of the characters. But where's the film leading? What does it want of me? A thirty-four-year old doctor with a stolen medical report in his briefcase which he'll be forced to return before he gets round to it. Or will he get round to it?

A stolen medical report in his briefcase. A farewell letter in his pocket.

I got the idea of the farewell letter from Martin. (It's important not to get held up putting pen to paper, in case you're in a terrible hurry.) He confided to me that he had always carried with him, in a stamped addressed envelope, a farewell letter to his aunt Agathe in Antibes, so that she would know whether he was alive or dead. (He was even careful, when he crossed the border into Germany on his long hike, to replace the French stamp on the envelope with a German one.) His life was such that he could never be sure of making it from one day to the next. And now it's come to the same stage with me as with dear Martin during his time as a beggar: a man with a farewell letter in his pocket.

And all set to betray Petra. Right from the start. Betrayal at first sight. All set to follow through with the betrayal once I had found her, and, at first sight also, had seen her as my wife.

PETRA'S AND MY six-month anniversary coincided with Martin's first day of chemotherapy. I had got as far as the parking area on my way home to drink champagne with Petra when I felt compelled to make a detour and drop in first at Martin's ward.

My patient was bearing up well, but said there was something very strange about his condition: he had acquired the yellow skin colour of the dead within ten minutes of them starting to pump the poison into him.

'With evil shall evil be cast out,' I said.

'And do you think it'll work?'

'I'm pretty sure it will, but I can't of course guarantee it.'

'So I might be subjecting myself to this horror for no other purpose than dying.'

'Well, you wouldn't be alone in that.'

'Do you think that's any consolation? '

'I don't know about a consolation. It's at least a fact. How are you finding it here at the hospital? '

'The staff are unbelievably good. They even find my German entertaining and they're patient with my babbling.'

'What you really need is an interpreter who you could always telephone.'

'An interpreter? '

'That's what I said. It could cost you dear if there were any doubt about the nature of your condition. Do you think it's an easy matter being ill in a foreign language? '

'For someone like me, who's hardly slept in a bed fit for humans in ten years, the important thing at present is the luxury of this bed. That, and, of course, the animal programmes on television. An elephant weighs a hundred kilos at birth: I saw that yesterday. It's something I'd completely forgotten.'

'What about the food?'

'You're no doubt worried that the cooking in a German hospital might kill a certain Frenchman if something else doesn't kill him first.'

'That's why I ask.'

'The food's perfectly okay. No complaints.'

'Is there anything you'd like me to bring you?'

'*Le Monde*, ideally. I used to sit in libraries for a good half-day at a time, going through *Le Monde*.'

I realised all of a sudden that I was sitting on Martin's bed. Normally I don't sit on my patients' beds. After we had looked one another straight in the eye in silence, I said: 'You were going to destroy yourself altogether, weren't you?'

'I ought to write a book about long-drawn out, unsuccessful attempts at suicide. I think my own experience must be quite unique. Whichever way I tried it, I was always rescued. On one occasion I lay down to sleep out of doors, carefully concealed behind some dustbins, with one cardboard sheet underneath me and another on top—not the best protection at seven below zero—and knew exactly what I was doing. I even got pneumonia as part of the plan. But would you believe it? There was some bastard of a rubbish collector who called the Paris police! They scooped me up and got me into a healthcare service bus. I was then transferred and driven to the hospital in style: in the finest of ambulances, bearing the sign *Réanimation*, 'Critical Care'. A clear case of generosity overdone!

'I tried various other tricks. But that was the nearest I got to finishing it once and for all. And when I got this cancer I felt so ill anyway that I gave up trying and looked around for some decent pain-killers at the first medical practice I could find, in Treptow of all places. The doctor was a rheumatologist. And not to make a long story of it, here I am, having fallen straight into the hands of the invincible Siegfried, the Tumour-Toppler!'

'Where does this self-destruction come from?'

'If our friendship is to continue you are not to ask such questions.'

'But you do know where it comes from?'

'Thanks for coming today,' said Martin, and turned his face to the wall.

'Listen, my friend,' I said, 'I meant you no disrespect. You've been in Berlin long enough now to know that we mean well, even if we don't always have the best of manners.'

Martin laughed coldly and said: 'Good manners are no guarantee that people are truly civilised.'

'As in the case of Hannibal Lecter?'

'Oh, cannibalism! That's nothing. That's child's play compared with some of the things people can turn their filthy minds to.'

I had written my mobile phone number on a piece of paper, and placed it on his bedside table, under the glass of water.

'Here's my mobile number,' I said. 'Will you at least ring me if I can do anything?'

'Thank you,' said Martin, and his voice seemed to break for a moment. He quickly made up for this, however, by turning towards me and giving me one of his most mischievous smiles.

I WAS IN low spirits as I drove home. What was it that lay heavy on my chest? My conversation with Martin?

Nothing should have come between me and the Yellow Widow, waiting as she was, cool and bubbling, in the fridge. I had planned to surprise Petra with a celebration of our half-year anniversary. But I was finding it impossible to put my heart and soul into the celebration. There was something I had to talk to her about, not of the happiest kind. It could wait no longer. Champagne would be altogether inappropriate for the conversation in question, so I would have to stop at the wine merchants' and buy some red wine, and get some cheese, biscuits and olives to replace the trout roe and blinis that I had bought to have with the champagne.

What was it that had got me into this state? Why was now the time for laying bare my soul and so wrecking my celebration with Petra? Was it the old familiar urge to self-destruction? And what had brought it on just now, when I was about to prove to my best and most dearly beloved how thrilled I was to have found her at the Ankerklause six months ago, and what a specialist I was in giving surprises?

'Cannibalism ... that's nothing ... *that's child's play compared with some of the things people can turn their filthy minds to*'. Was it the words CHILD'S PLAY that had given me such a nudge that I did not want to let a day pass without telling Petra the truth?

The truth? Well, not the whole truth. If I told her that

she would not be seeing her husband but rather a little boy coming home from school every day and turning aside into the big park where there is a man with a bright red yo-yo. He holds it and lets go, holds and lets go, and looks up with a friendly smile and gestures to me to come and join him where he's sitting by the cascading brook, holding and letting go, holding and letting go, and there's a black birthmark on his index finger. He gestures to me again to come and join him, with an even bigger smile, and I was on my way to the brook anyway to take off my shoes and socks and dip my toes in the water.

And this funny man offers me a go with his yo-yo, and he's telling me that he has a nice little yo-yo factory in his garage, and when I'm there I'll be able to choose a yellow, a red, a green or a blue yo-yo. I'll choose a red one.

ALTHOUGH I DON'T like having children near me, or talking to them or touching them, there have been times, when the conditions were right, as on a few occasions at the Brachvogel, that I've watched them while they were playing and could see what struggling bundles of fun some children are at the ages of two or three, how inventive they are in their games, how they can be cruel one minute and kind the next, innocent and cunning at the same time, and that someone who has no children is missing a lot. And

I've never forgotten little Petra, Mikki's sister, whose coal-black hair I could pat and stroke, who kissed me on the cheek and said she wanted to marry me when she grew up, and I said Yes, we'll make sure we do that when we're grown up. And as for the other Petra, my own Petra, I'll never know whether she had really had enough of looking after her brother in the family home with a mentally ill mother and is content to have no children of her own, or whether she's living only half a life with me because we don't have any. I catch myself looking into her make-up bag in the mornings to make sure she's remembered to take her pill. On one occasion when she'd forgotten to do so I was on tenterhooks throughout the day and was thinking of ringing her to remind her to take it. But what excuse could I find for rummaging through her things, what would I be looking for in a make-up bag containing lipstick and night cream? When I looked again in the evening she had put things to rights.

A BORDEAUX THAT I knew to be particularly good and not exorbitantly priced was still on sale, fortunately, at the wine merchants' in the street next to the hospital, and I also paid a visit to Galeries Lafayette to get three sorts of cheese to which Martin had made a big thing of introducing me.

Petra saw as soon as I walked in the door that I wasn't

my usual self. It's not just that she's brighter than I am; she has a means of knowing, as if by radar, how people are feeling, and she manages somehow to see to it that this super-sense never becomes oppressive. Someone said that what intelligence amounts to is sensitivity, and after my years with Petra I can only agree.

Naturally, I had already opened the bottle. It was the same excellent wine as last time, so that at least was no problem.

'Are we celebrating our half-year? ' asked Petra.

'Of course we are,' I said. 'But I have something serious to say to you at the same time. It suddenly struck me today that I can't put it off any longer.'

'Cheers,' said Petra, 'and congratulations to us, on our half-year! I look forward to celebrating the whole year.'

So we drank our health and Petra kissed me as only she knows how to do. How mortal men would envy me if they knew what a choice bestower of kisses I am privileged to live with! And perhaps they would weep also if they knew that my heart remains unmoved even though my brain recognises how deeply felt the kisses are. And so perfectly formed is this robot that is me that even super-sensitive Petra with her sixth sense doesn't know the difference between it and a living being. My most terrifying nightmares are about Petra finding out that it's not human blood that runs in my veins but rather some ghastly, indescribable, robotic liquid.

And Petra disengaged herself from the robot's claws, looked into its inorganic eyes and asked: 'What is it?'

'It's difficult,' I said. 'It's a matter of grave concern that I have to raise with you. An existential matter. Serious stuff.'

'Matters of grave concern don't scare me.'

'I know you're not easily scared.'

'It's an occupational disease. From my upbringing.'

I couldn't help laughing at the number of things that come into Petra's head. I fell silent then and wondered how on earth I was going to continue this sick man's account of himself while giving the impression that all was well— something that with Petra of all people, with her long experience of mental illness, was hardly likely to succeed.

She came to my aid. 'Do go on,' she said, 'Tell me about it, whatever it is. That's what I'm here for.'

'It's all the more difficult because it's half absurd. But if you could see what I'm going to say in the light of the admission that I love you, that I want to be with you until I die …'

'Or until I do,' she interrupted me.

'God forbid,' I said, in English. 'As I was saying, until I die …'

'Go on,' said Petra.

'The problem is that I'm not an altogether normal product.'

'That's no great news,' said Petra. 'That may be a problem for you, but it isn't for me.'

'Hold on now. I have to tell you something that may cause you deep disappointment and might ruin everything. It's been troubling me since our very first day together, whether I should tell you about it then, which might have been the kindest thing to do, to give you the chance to find someone better straight away. You haven't fled yet, thank God, but I find I really can't keep silent any longer.'

Petra was looking at me not as if she was surprised, but as if she knew in advance what I was going to say and was simply waiting for its confirmation. She allowed me to remain silent and gather strength.

I was trying to feel my way carefully forward with what I wanted to say. 'It's half absurd really. But only half. If that.'

Petra went on looking at me patiently, while I steeled myself to letting it out.

'As I've said, I want to spend my life with you.'

'That's mutual, as you know.'

'Perhaps it won't be mutual when I've told you something about myself, something which has been clear to me for a very long time and is not going to change.'

'So what is it?'

'I can't see myself having children.'

'Well, you're right: that's something I need to know.'

'But shouldn't I have told you this before?'

'That's alright, you're telling me now.'

'But what do you think?'

'Looking at the overall picture, it's not by any means certain that you could have children if you wanted to. Or that I could. There are many people who can't have children at all.'

'Are you saying that you're taking this all in the day's work?'

'Why not? How else should I be taking it?'

'Shouldn't you be asking yourself if you want to have children?'

'I don't know that I would have wanted to. But the point is that I no longer need to consider the question. I'm going to live with you till death us do part, and if children are not part of the package, so be it.'

'I don't understand the way you're taking this.'

'It's not about me, it's about you. You've given me this information, you've told me that that's part of how you are, and that's it. The fact that you are as you say you are, in this case that you don't want to have children, is something I take seriously. I want be with you, with no holds barred, as you are. I can't be with you as you aren't! It's you, from top to toe, that has pride of place. And children or no children, that's how it must be. It's not complicated; it's simply a question of priorities.'

'But what about your feelings? What about your fulfilment in life?'

'You are my fulfilment in life. And remember that I might not have wanted children myself, or not without discussing it. Now I no longer need to consider the question. It'll save me a bit of energy!'

'But after ten years, when your time for bearing children runs out, what then?'

'I'm not looking ten years ahead. We'll cross that bridge when we come to it. But by then there'll be even less space in our lives for a child. A child needs space. It's awful to see people having children and not having space for them, either in terms of time or in their hearts. As for me, having had to take my mother's place in looking after my brother, I think I've had enough of looking after children to last me a lifetime. Someone with my upbringing is not really a child person.'

'You've never told me this.'

'It's simply never come up. Thank you for taking the initiative. To be perfectly honest with you, I'm almost relieved that the ruling in this matter has been taken out of my hands.'

'It wasn't a ruling, it was an arbitrary exercise of power.'

'I know you well enough to know that you're not doing this just for fun. And I also know you well enough to know that you won't change your mind.'

'That's true enough.'

'So I know what I'm going along with. It's great to have a husband who comes clean on such basic questions. It's a privilege, and not such a common one, to know where you stand with your husband.'

'To this extent you know it, at least!'

'To this extent, yes! But could it be that you're keeping

a certain ice-cold widow hidden away? Where do I stand with you as far as she's concerned?'

'I was planning to celebrate our half-year anniversary. But I didn't think champagne would go with what I was going to tell you.'

'I have a suggestion,' said Petra. 'Stick the cork back in the bottle of red: it'll keep; and let's celebrate with champagne the fact that we're going to live in blissful freedom from screaming kids and dirty nappies for the rest of our lives. What is there to celebrate if not that? Just think how many more yellow widows it will add to our lives!'

'Fair point,' I said, got up, went to the fridge and prepared a champagne celebration with the trout roe and blinis. Then I went to the lavatory with no other purpose than to flush the loo and turn on the taps, and the salt water from my eyes ran together with the tap water.

I BREATHE MORE easily once I've parked the car outside the hospital grounds. A safe haven at last. Though there have been cases of my being disturbed in the car, by some hard-pressed secretary, or a patient in dire straits, knocking on the window.

My briefcase with the auburn-haired girl's medical records is on the front seat beside me. Can I really believe that I have done this?

This seems to be the way it happens. You start by doing something silly like lifting a document from the psychiatric ward, and once you're over that threshold you can just as easily go on, over more thresholds and higher ones. Who's to know in what uncharted territory such a hurdle race will end?

The argument in favour of what I've done is as watertight as any arch-villain would claim. I couldn't start reading these pages on the spot, when I was in the psychiatric ward. Why then didn't I sneak up to my own department to photocopy the file there, and then replace the original? Because I truly didn't have the strength to do any photocopying today. Watertight excuses, these, for taking the file out to my car. It can hardly be considered pilfering as long as the document remains within the hospital grounds, can it? And then you drive out through the gate without seeming to notice where you've gone.

There remain the unanswered questions of where and when to read it, whether the report has been pilfered or not. I want plenty of time to go over every word, even though I know what's in it. But for the moment I'm not up to reading anything, and I wouldn't have the time anyway, as I've got to start picking my way home to dear Petra before too much time elapses.

It makes me feel uncomfortable, pilfering a confidential document: dishonest, unprofessional. And what would happen in the unlikely event of Petra looking into my briefcase and finding it? She would conclude at once that her husband the doctor had become a case for treatment. She's someone who takes the confidentiality of nursing so seriously that it's quite an event if she tells me anything about her work, and she never mentions names.

I ring Petra to announce that I'm on my way to the rosé wine and cheese puffs and she responds warmly, saying that there's still some faint light on the balcony, that we can easily sit outside with sweaters on, and that we really should get round to buying a gas heater.

I must remember this: to leave my briefcase behind in the car so that there's no risk of Petra happening upon my ill-gotten document, in the unlikely event of her needing to look in my briefcase.

IN ONE PART of my mind I'm looking forward to getting onto the balcony with Petra and watching the twin trees, so soon turning green, that shelter the graves of Sommer and Luft from the weather of all seasons: from sunshine, snow, and the winds; and to sharing with Petra my joy that spring has come, even though this spring day is virtually over; and there'll be plenty of time to do my reading when Petra, sleepy as night approaches, lays her head on her pillow; plenty of time to be on my own with the psychiatric ward's report on the auburn-haired girl that was, and who is now a faded wreck scattering flowers on the pavement from the first floor and laughing her rusty laugh in the glaring sun.

Petra has no idea that we live just a stone's throw away from the parents who adopted me up there, Sommer and Luft. This delightful couple were unmarried here on earth, but found one another in a new and better place and took into their care a boy who was having dreadful problems without any one knowing it but himself, this boy who was named Montag down there on earth but SommerLuft from then onwards. And not Martin but Mikki. SommerLuft. Mikki SommerLuft.

And that boy there who comes home from school one fine day and runs into a man with a bright red yo-yo in a park with a smooth-flowing cascade, he's been coming home from school every day since then. He's not permitted to leave youth behind like other people, he's stuck fast in the day when he came home from school and in that regard he'll never become an adult; he has to muddle along in an endless state of childishness. So he's in the right place, in the city which, according to lengthy pronouncements by Martin, is *the city of sufferings*:

'I FELT I was on to a good thing here as soon as I arrived,' says Martin. 'Berlin is the ideal place for a homeless person: he blends in with the crowd easily. It's inappropriate, somehow, for waifs and strays to live in that magnificent, untouchable, unspoilt city of Paris: it's as if the homeless are upsetting the city by living with such gay abandon in a place where nothing that's worth calling bad has ever happened.'

I would normally allow my friend to ramble on in his monologues and enjoy listening to them, but here I felt the need to be serious.

'Hold on, are you sure you're quite right in the head? What do you mean by saying that nothing that's worth calling bad has ever happened in your favourite city? Weren't any Jews ever transported *en masse* from Paris to their deaths? With unforgivable collaboration by the locals? Weren't the streets and squares ever channels for streams of blood in the revolution?'

'I'm not counting the revolution, it's so long ago. And I'm not making light of the forced transportation of the Jews or the collaboration by the French. By some of the French. But remember that the French resistance movement is the finest such movement that has ever been formed, so it's not just cowards we're talking about, but heroes, yes, heroes!'

'You know what a French snob I am. I need no encouragement in that.'

'I'm talking about an entire, unspoilt, magnificent city as opposed to a city that has been blown apart. A city of mountainous ruins, starving people, indescribable suffering. Suffering undergone by the old, the sick, the wounded, and by children. Two million women raped.

'It would be appalling bad taste to make a comedy film about Berlin in the second world war. But to judge from French films you might think that Paris had simply waltzed through the war with no more to worry about than where the next succulent steak was coming from, as in *La Traversée de Paris*. That's a film you should see: it stars Jean Gabin and Louis de Funès and it's about the problems of smuggling a freshly slaughtered pig in suitcases from one part of Paris to another at a time when the war was at its worst. You simply must see it: there's a DVD of it. And there are also films about the resistance movement, with torture scenes, it's true, but also showing a glass of red wine and a baguette, my friend, with a nice piece of cheese thrown in if such a thing can be rustled up from somewhere, so that the city-dwellers under occupation see light in the darkness and the down-and-outs have cause for rejoicing.

'But that doesn't alter the fact that the homeless person in Paris is a blot on the landscape and shouldn't really be there. In Berlin he's part of the furniture. Most people look as though they're homeless anyway, squatters and artists and so on, and that's the good thing about being here, you don't stand out. And that's very important: who wants to go around with a label stuck on him? In France you stand out if you've got two days' stubble on your face; in Berlin you stand out if you've shaved. There's something not right about you: you're an oddball or an official, one or the other.

'In Berlin the homeless and the down-and-outs are taken for granted. There are shelters, laundrettes, and restaurants in the centre of town where a plate of food costs practically nothing. And that's as it should be: it's better for the soul to pay out a few symbolic coins than to pay nothing at all.'

'Then I'm very proud of the way these things are handled in my native city.'

'You should be,' was Martin's refrain, before he launched into a further account of his earlier life.

'Many people think there's no method to the life of a down-and-out, but that's not true. If you don't plan, you're dead before you know it, with nothing to drink, nothing to eat, no warm grid to sleep on, no cardboard box to doss down in. And you need to be well on top of things if you want to stay anyway clean. There were no laundrettes for down-and-outs in my Paris years. Nowhere to brush your teeth, have a shower, shave or get your hair cut.

'I always made sure my hair was well cut. It never occurred to me to use scissors on my hair myself, or to let friends do it. I ingratiated myself with barbers in some of the dingier streets and would turn up in the mornings when everything was quiet and get my hair cut every single month. Usually free of charge.

'It's very important for a down-and-out not to be ugly. I didn't really look anything like a homeless person, but more like someone who was just a little drunk and possibly love-sick. I played on being an object of pity, and this worked best with older women's hearts. It was the motherly ones who kept me breathing. Young women are cruel and think of nothing but themselves: someone down on his luck will only be a burden to them, but it came naturally to older women, who probably had sons who were failures or mother's boys, to do things for me. I suppose they felt they were doing something for their beloved son.

'I always had washing stuff with me in my backpack: toothbrush, toothpaste, and shaving kit, and I would wait for an opportunity to nip into a place where I could shave without being got at and brush my teeth in peace. I made sure I got in with several cafés where there was bound to be hot water in the taps, and would shave in the Gents of one of them, and then another. Always with permission. All you need is permission. Start shaving somewhere without it and they'll call the police. But just ask if you can shave and they might even give you a clean towel! The procedure is to make a habit of going to the place, sometimes without buying anything because you haven't a bean to your name, ask if you can just sit for a bit in the warm and be careful not to stay too long, look at a paper, wait for someone to start a conversation with you rather than be the first to get people talking, and you end up being given the occasional espresso, perhaps even half a baguette, maybe even with butter. Especially if it's an older woman serving and you could be her son, that's the best scenario. I had two mothers like that from the tavern world, both in the Eighteenth Arrondissement, close by the Chateau Rouge; one was black, from Cameroon. This one wasn't old at all, really. We had rules: I could stay with her if it was colder than five degrees below freezing; then I could use her shower and sleep in her bed. And I could also use her phone to ring my aunt in Antibes, who sent me money, so I took the good lady from Cameroon out to dinner! She had various tricks up her sleeve, this good lady: for example she sent me to a friend of hers who sold second-hand clothes. He fitted me out with the gladdest of rags, a red sweater, for instance, which reached down to my knees, and I'm convinced that ruin of a sweater kept the breath of life in me for a whole month of February. A free sweater! And fortunately also a free overcoat to cover the wretched thing: wearing a woman's red sweater reaching down to my knees would hardly have helped me in asking for favours like having a haircut! That would have meant the down-and-out, or the suffering lover, or whatever, becoming a freak that no-one would want anywhere near them. For a down-and-out, clothes and keeping clean are key factors for survival, much more important than clothing is for other classes of person, because a tramp's life depends on his not getting that side of things wrong. If he does, then he's *persona non grata*. A well turned out, reasonably smelling down-and-out in passable clothes could easily be a love-sick person on a temporary drinking binge. Love-sickness can happen to anybody. The idea that a reasonable-looking young man can be so deeply sensitive that love drags him down into the gutter makes a touching, attractive impression.

'The main thing for the homeless person is to learn what people are like: his life depends on it. One thing he learns is that "people" and "people" can mean very different things. It's as though people and people are different kinds of animal. I learnt that lesson very early on in my life.'

'When, then, and how?' I asked.

Martin fell silent and looked at me questioningly, as though into a crystal ball. I thought to myself how I should have been the one doing that.

'What are you hinting at about lessons learnt early on in the course of your life?'

Martin remained silent and smiled as Buster Keaton might have done, if Buster Keaton had smiled. He continued in his silent pose until I resumed the theme of Berlin and told him straight out that I had hardly thought of Berlin as the city of sufferings.

'But you've always lived here. Who ever gives much thought to the city where he lives? We take our home town for granted. And comparison with Paris is beyond you.'

'I've often been there, as you know. Paris is my second city.'

'But you haven't lived there, you don't know the little restaurants where you can get real French food for next to nothing but where no tourist would ever dream of going; you haven't had, as your daily bread, a newly baked baguette with exactly the right crust thickness, and a properly made croissant with apricot jam along with your cup of espresso, before the day's drinking begins.'

'We eat muesli and yoghourt at my place. It's healthier than that white bread and jam. I allow myself orange marmalade only on Sundays.'

'My God, muesli! I might have known it. That powdery, gritty stuff makes me quite sick. It's for a Stone Age stomach.'

'Muesli is a Swiss invention.'

'There's a lot of that in Berlin: muesli, ruins, and powdered grit. The suffering is still there in Berlin, you see it in people's faces, just look at them on the street, you see the last days of the war in the city, it's indescribable: hangings, rapes, and children playing soldiers in defence of the country even after all was lost; nor was there any let-up in the suffering after the war, when the city was divided in two by this incomprehensible German wall which followed no laws of geometry, worming its way endlessly through the city in a zig-zag line. Even people like me who have studied this one-time wall—for I had little to do apart from studying the wall here before I met you—even a wall-specialist like me hadn't the faintest idea whether I was in former East or West Berlin at any particular street corner. And the suffering went on even though the war was over, I don't need to tell you that, an unheard-of situation in one and the same city, people getting shot at short range like beasts in a slaughterhouse if they tried to escape the bliss of the Eastern Bloc, and the east side authorities watching children from the west drown in the canal rather than run the risk of the enemy entering their territory to save a child. To save a child!'

'Yes,' I said. 'Odd that you should mention that. My one friend died that way, my Turkish friend Mikki. I never had any other friend until I met you.'

'Why have you never told me this?' asked Martin, amazed.

'There's quite a bit I haven't told you,' I said.

'I don't doubt that,' he said. 'It's mutual, in fact.'

'Right enough, you've not told me about that surname you got rid of.'

'To name just one example,' he said.

'And what was this about "people" and "people" meaning different things, and lessons learnt early on in the course of your life?'

'There was that too,' he said.

'Yes. The fact is that I don't know much about you from before you became a down-and-out, before you were even twenty.'

'Like the fact that I don't know much about you when you were young and growing up in Berlin.'

'That's true enough,' I said.

'Who knows?' said Martin, 'maybe we'll tell each other a

few things one of these fine days.'

'That fine day will never come,' I said, 'not for me.'

'I understand,' said Martin.

'No you don't,' I said.

And Martin looked at me with a curious, searching look, and he might as well have gone on staring at me for ever: I just sat there and presented an impenetrable wall to his gaze.

Thus it is that bosom friends sit and talk, well into their lives if they're spared, without ever getting to the heart of the matter. Or is it friendship itself that is the heart of the matter, the fact of having a soul-mate? It doesn't seem to be the friend's experience of life, or not directly.

MARTIN RESPONDED BADLY to the chemotherapy. With the second round of treatment he became so thin that he was unrecognisable. As bald as an egg, his face shrunken, his eyes dull, his nose protruding and beak-like. By the end of the session his blood cell count had gone down so far that I felt I had no alternative but to have him put into hospital. He protested violently, but I did not give in.

I skipped lunch and went to see him in the ward. Jadwiga was with him. I had never seen her before. Although I had never doubted that Martin's descriptions of her were accurate, seeing truly is believing. This highly articulate

Frenchman had simply not found the words, and perhaps there were no words, to describe how this woman moved, in a gentle, Slavic rhythm, how graceful her mouth was when she talked, and how she had arranged her hair in an elegant, loosely tied knot.

I fell for her at once and without hesitation, head over heels, and did not feel in any way guilty. On the contrary, I took pleasure in the fact that Martin's best beloved should have this effect on me. (There was no question of a bad conscience in relation to Petra; she wasn't part of this.) This wild love at first sight was a divine gift, and that was how I saw it: a divine gift and a total secret, precious and delightful.

I would never touch this woman, and what luck it was for this robot to be in love with a woman he would never touch, did not want to touch, was not allowed to touch! This love did not detract from my love for Petra, it added to it. After meeting Jadwiga I would be better able than before to love the divine gift I had at home with all the resources available to a robot.

There in the ward with Jadwiga and Martin I had been sucked in under the shelter of their love and was lingering there, invisible but at the same time an active participant, deeply in love with the same woman as my soul-mate. And Martin was in such a state of elation that it seemed altogether as though he had laid the thin, bald covering of his body aside, allowing his soul to engage in a dance beyond the reach of all harms.

I was moved to tears and needed to blow my nose. They could see what my feelings were and handled it well, both giving me, in civilised manner, a smile of happiness, and holding hands like two nursery school children at story time.

Then it struck me that something special was in the air that day, as though I was going to hear news of great consequence, and I forgot for the moment that I was in love with the woman in the ward who spoke my native language so well, with her beautiful mouth and delightful accent.

I began to feel really worried about whatever was afoot, and wasn't able to conceal it. I felt I should leave rather than hang around like an idiot. Then Jadwiga said she had to go to work, so I stayed on.

She bade me farewell with an angelic kiss. I felt as if I had been touched for the first time: it hadn't happened before, not like that, and I was shaken to the roots like a buffeted apple tree.

Then she had gone, leaving behind in the ward a mysterious whiff of something which, it turned out, was some Polish herbal broth she had brought for Martin.

I brought the chair up to the bed and asked how he was doing.

'It doesn't matter', he said, and smiled like a yogi sitting on a post.

'It would help the doctor to know how you're feeling.'

'I think I'm pretty weak.'

'Does it hurt anywhere in particular?'

'I've got a terrible mouth ulcer, so can only take liquids; it's best through a straw. May I tell you something?'

'Of course,' I said.

But I didn't want to hear what he was going to say, and I looked away like someone expecting not the best of news.

Martin looked at me apologetically. I felt as though my life were taking an unexpected turn, and indeed as if I were going to die on the spot because of this, as if all the moments of my existence were gathering together into one, and the last one, because of what was coming.

Martin continued to look at me apologetically. I was so out of control that he would clearly have avoided speaking if he could, but there was no turning back, he was compelled to tell me his news, given the way things were.

'I would have to tell you this sometime in any case,' he said, and he had already started sounding as though he had done something wrong.

I gave him a sidelong glance. He was studying the sleeve of his nightshirt very closely, though there was neither a stain nor a crease on it, far less anything resembling a mystical sign.

'It's Jadwiga,' he said. 'Jadwiga.'

He fell silent after this brief declaration, as if he did not have the strength to continue. There was a frail quality to his voice.

After a short time he said: 'No. It's not just her. It's us, the two of us, as you might say. We're expecting a baby.'

'Wha-at?'

Martin looked at me, and yes, his face radiated pity. (Not surprisingly.)

'You heard right. We're expecting a baby.'

'But you said you were never going to have a child. You said that, you did!'

'Well, that's what's happened. And we're happy.'

'That's all too evident.'

Martin was silent and his look of pity increased.

'But how are the two of you going to cope?' I asked, and I couldn't conceal the rage that was surging up within me from the depths of my being. 'How are you going to manage, with a child that's born while, in the worst case scenario, you're helpless.'

'Have no worries on that score, *mon ami*.' This was the first time he had called me a friend in his mother tongue. I found that very moving, and those two words, *mon ami*, checked the torrent of rage that was surging within me. I simply sat there where I was, in my so-called lunch break, gradually assimilating this appalling news. Appalling for whom? The truth was that I was not in my right mind; my friend could no longer be expected to doubt that.

'We've got good family support, Martin. Jadwiga has a mother, two sisters and two brothers, and my aunt in Antibes will come up trumps with the bank when she hears about the baby. That's if her heart stands the strain of such joyful news. We've started to plan. During the birth and the first month, and for longer if need be, Jadwiga's mother and her sister will take turns to be with us. And I'm keeping on my room at the church so I won't have to be constantly in people's way.'

'You shouldn't count on being able to manage on your own, either in that room or anywhere else, in another six months or so.'

'None of your pessimism, thanks.'

'You're not responding well to the treatment, and you've got two more rounds to go.'

'No more pessimism, thanks. I'm sure I'm not going to go on responding badly.'

Martin fell silent and closed his eyes. I could see now that I had hurt him. Of course I had hurt him.

'You must forgive the way I'm taking this,' I said. 'I'm not in control of myself. I've got a thing about those little horrors.'

Martin opened his eyes and looked at me: 'You're a strange mixture,' he said.

'You could say that, ' I said, my mouth as dry as desert sand.

Martin was silent and I continued:

'This child phobia is so bad that I couldn't face doing my stint in the paediatric ward when I was studying. The Vice-Chair of the Medical Faculty spared me this by signing a cooked-up document saying that I was suffering from paedophobia: fear of children. It's a condition that hardly exists, except perhaps in the case of the captain in *Star Trek*.'

'Would you care to tell me this intriguing story in detail? You've just said a whole lot in far too few words.'

I naturally indulged my friend by telling him the story, to pass the time for him and by way of excusing myself for my extreme reaction to his news. An inexcusable reaction. But not inexplicable. The story is as follows:

I HAD MANAGED by various ruses to avoid working in the paediatric ward. But now I could get out of it no longer. It was clear that I would fall behind and not be allowed to take my finals until I had done my stint in the children's ward like any other medical student. I had to do something about it, and quick; there was nothing for it but to go to the top.

I didn't want to talk to the Chair of the Faculty, a veteran of the Herr-Professor-Doktor school, but the Vice-Chair, Ottenmaier, or Otti as we called him, was in tune with the modern age. Tall and slim, and something of a comedian, he was as handsome as a film star, of the Cary Grant type. A surgeon who had put aside the scalpel to study psychiatry: the only example I know of such a sudden, and admirable, change of heart. Surgeons are necessary, I suppose, in the cases with which they deal, but they're an altogether ghastly class of person. It's not always a matter of pure chance where people find jobs, and there's a pretty high percentage of sadists in the surgical profession. Their tendency is to cut away too much. This has been demonstrated scientifically.

Well, I came straight to the point with Ottenmaier, and said I was having serious difficulties with my studies.

'There's no sign of that in your grades or teachers' reports. Your reports and grades are exemplary. Hard to find better.'

I then came out with it straight away: that I had put off doing my stint in the children's ward. And now the day of reckoning had come. There was a danger that completion of my finals would be delayed as a result.

Otti gave me a questioning, highly suspicious look. He remained silent, so I had to press on regardless.

'I'm afraid of children,' I said. 'I can't bear the thought of being near children. The very words, *children's ward*, make everything go black before my eyes.'

'So that's all it is? We can fix that easily.'

I'll never forget the look with which he accompanied those words. He looked straight through me.

'Thank you,' I said. 'Such an eccentricity could, at worst, ruin one's career.'

'An eccentricity, yes. What happened?'

'I've simply never got to know children; I was born old. I wouldn't dare to pick up a little child for fear of harming it.

And it wouldn't be right for me to have patients who can't express themselves. I wouldn't know how to handle them. I know my limits.'

'So you'd never have made a vet,' said Otti, with a laugh.

'That least of all,' I lied. (I have sometimes regretted not becoming a vet. Maybe it's not too late to do so.)

Otti took out some departmental stationery, wrote three lines on a sheet of paper, and asked me to read them.

This is to certify that I, Martin Montag, medical student, suffer from a rare psychiatric disorder, paedophobia, or fear of children, and am consequently exempted from duties in the paediatric ward, subject to the approval of the Faculty Board.

'I've never heard of this phobia, paedophobia,' I said.

'It's not unknown,' said Otti, running his hand through his hair in the way that Cary Grant surely did in *North by Northwest*. 'The captain in *Star Trek* had a fear of children, and had to ask one of his underlings to take care of any children who had sneaked on board. He admitted he was afraid of children.'

'I'm relieved to hear I'm not the only person in the world who's dogged by this problem.'

'We hardly ever are,' said Otti and smiled again.

'I don't know how to thank you,' I said.

'Thank yourself. If you'd been a dunce things would have been altogether different. But your brilliance is such that the rules have to be set aside. And from my point of view it's a thousand times better that you should come to me and tell me honestly about this difficulty than that you should go and work in the paediatric ward and be a fish out of water. That might have made a difference to your final grade, something I regard as very important.'

'You can't be afraid that mine will be better than yours!'

'No, I don't fear that, though it looks as though it will be. But I don't mind being the loser when the winner is of your calibre.'

To this very day I remember how he talked to me, wet behind the ears as I was, as an equal. I've found this to be the case with more than one of the truly eminent people I have met: that they don't sit on their high horse. They don't need to because they're on it already and they bring you up to their level. Otti is one of those people who raises the level of those he's talking to.

It occurred to me to ask what would happen to the document, with its diagnosis of paedophobia.

'I'll stamp it as "confidential" and tuck it away somewhere in the archives. It would not be ideal if a phobia of this order of magnitude got misplaced in the system!' And Otti laughed.

I joined in with only a faint laugh, worried about how the Faculty Board would react. Did he think it likely that the Board would buy this diagnosis? Paedophobia?

'I'll do my best,' he said. 'We're fortunate in that our esteemed chairman will be absent from the next meeting but one, so I'll bring it up then, acting for him in this matter. My prediction is that it'll be alright. There's a bit of snobbery about first-class students like yourself. I'm pretty sure they'll all agree to smoothing the way for someone who's all set to take on the toughest of struggles in the fight to save human lives. Am I right in thinking that you plan to brandish the ray gun?'

'Yes, that's right.'

'I'm glad. You have the temperament for it.'

And with that I left, not without a touch of pleasure and pride. And that's it, Monsieur Martinetti.

'These Germans are always more craftily colourful than one thinks,' said Martin, and gave a long, ugly, cough-racked laugh which had been welling up inside him with a wheezing sound while I was talking. I wanted to reach for the stethoscope, but did not think it right to let medicine intrude on this private conversation.

It was downright despicable the way I had taken this miraculous, joyful news: the woman had succeeded in becoming pregnant with things the way they were and would not have the chance again, not with her beloved Martin, after his treatment for cancer. As for me, I was supposed to be a doctor yet had put my foot in it so disgracefully. The best thing for me was to keep quiet, to be thoroughly ashamed of myself, and to listen carefully to the sound level of my patient's coughing.

When Martin had to some extent recovered he said:

'I never intended to have children, any more than you do, as I've told you. But it's a bit unreasonable of you to carry on as if Jadwiga becoming pregnant is some sort of betrayal. She intended it to happen, I'm sure of it.'

'It's just not possible to intend such a thing. Not just like that.' (I could hear the bad-tempered tone in my voice. Watch out!)

'It's no ordinary person we're talking about, remember. This is Jadwiga.'

I could only agree with him whole-heartedly on that point: that my new-found beloved was in no way ordinary. With that I left, making my way, bowled over, baffled, and bewildered, to my hideaway, after a prolonged midday break. It was then, out on the terrace, that I ran into the patient with the IV drip stand who was smoking, and all but knocked him over and set fire to my coat.

THOSE CHEESE PUFFS of Petra's, made from my mother's recipe, have never gone down better and the rosé wine is well up to the standard of last time: we say 'Cheers' and wish one another a joyful spring! Our balcony is resplendent with candles in lanterns, lighting up the black tulips which have started to nod their heads at the end of the day, and there we sit, like a king and queen of the living, with a view of the land of the dead on the other side of the street.

À propos of the best cheese puffs in the world, Petra asks if we shouldn't invite my mother and father to a meal at the weekend; but I'm not in the mood for that. Petra reminds me that I'm never in the mood for seeing them and I feel a pang of conscience about this. She says she's not trying to make me feel guilty but my parents naturally regret the fact that our contact with them is so sporadic: we should manage things better, not least because I'm lucky enough not to have a mentally ill mother, and I say yes, I admit I'm out of line and I'm ashamed of it, I really will pull my socks up, but not this weekend because I'm dead tired and may be getting a cold. Then Petra says we'll just take it easy and might go to the seaside on Sunday, if I'm fit, to get a head start on the birthday celebrations as it's my birthday on Monday, and I say 'Yes, why not? Seaside on Sunday because birthday on Monday,' and I remember now that I've got a farewell letter to Petra folded in the breast pocket of my shirt, which is not the safest place for such a document. It's not certain that I'll live to see this birthday, and I take a sidelong glance at Martin Montag who has started to go downhill, Martin Montag who has become *a danger to himself and to others*. Downhill, not only because he has a stolen medical report in his briefcase outside in the car, but also because he has a farewell letter, not in an envelope, in his breast pocket.

Darkness falls. The twin trees on the graves of Sommer and Luft can now hardly be seen, and it's no longer warm enough to be sitting outside. Petra asks if we shouldn't think of going out to dinner, but I say no, citing my on-coming cold as an excuse, and Petra, considerate as ever, asks if I wouldn't then like to lie down while she's getting dinner ready.

So I take a nap on the sofa and in the half-light there's no-one present: I'm alone in the world with the shadows of crosses thrown on the walls by the window-posts as the lights of cars go by. Crosses are my friends: there'll be a cross above me when I'm dead, and then I'll no longer be on my way home from school. Dead, that's the best thing to be. Then everything will be as it was before I went home from school.

Petra doesn't fuss me when I'm out of sorts. I allow my-self long periods of silence when I'm in that kind of mood, and Petra remains unaffected. It's particularly fitting that the demands of companionship are not pressing upon us this evening.

It's not for any happy reason, of course, that my dear Petra is patient with me. The first, second, and third com-mandments for a child brought up by a mentally ill moth-er are patience, patience, patience. And I still find myself wondering if the essential trick in choosing a spouse is to find someone who is clever enough to tolerate one's weak-nesses.

I TRY NEVER to break the habit of making Saturday visits to Petra's mother. Petra and I usually go separately so as to make more visits in total. I sit with her for a long time, something like two to three hours, and Petra admires my stamina, all the more so as her Martin is a restless character. I usually go on Saturdays after looking in at the hospital, after swimming. It's not till after the visit that Petra's and my weekend begins, when quite a bit of Saturday has gone.

It wasn't just to make myself attractive to Petra that I came to develop a fondness for her mother: I genuinely sympathised with this pitiable figure. I felt it must be possible to raise her spirits by some means or other. I looked at medical records, spoke to her doctor, consulted the psychiatrists at my hospital. This led to new drugs being tried; she was put on a programme to build up her neglected physical condition, starting with swimming exercises. The result was that her health, both mental and physical, improved appreciably in only six months, and she was looking once again like a human being. It was possible to go out for a stroll with her, for instance. And whether or not her mental state really had improved she could sometimes give the impression of being quite normal. That was probably the most one could hope for. You could sometimes keep a conversation going with her for as long as ten minutes before she lapsed into incoherent babbling or weeping.

I enjoy talking about books and literature with her. Her favourites are Thomas Mann and Rilke. She still has a clear idea of *The Magic Mountain* and *The Duino Elegies* even after long years of mental illness, and she keeps them beside her on her bedside table, as a reassurance, from one year to the next, whether she's reading them or not. In her best moments one can talk to her about her companions Mann and Rilke as if she were a leading authority on both.

She sometimes also retells her mother's and father's stories from the war years. The stories are often the same, but I'm not averse to listening to them again and again, and sometimes a question put at the right moment can trigger off a story I haven't heard before and can bring important themes to light. It's in the details that such themes lie hidden, as any radiologist—or artist—knows.

Again and again I've heard her tell the story of Petra's grandmother. She was an old woman who had lost her husband when she at last told what had happened to her in the war. The same as what had happened to two million women in Berlin: raped by their saviours, the Russian soldiers. She was pregnant and took the risk of having an abortion, performed by the methods of the time. She said she would rather die than have a child as a result of rape. And she very nearly did die. And she had carried this secret, this horror, with her all her life without ever once mentioning it. When she was asked if the burden of silence had been heavy on top of the appalling event itself, she replied that it would have been a still heavier burden to talk about it, and inconceivable while her husband was alive. But now that

I'm an old woman, she had said, I want my people to know my story, I want them to remember the human being that I am, and was, with all the relevant facts, including the worst thing that happened to me and almost cost me my life.

... TO REMEMBER THE HUMAN BEING THAT I AM, AND WAS, WITH ALL THE RELEVANT FACTS, INCLUDING THE WORST THING THAT HAPPENED TO ME AND ALMOST COST ME MY LIFE.

She was of sound mind throughout her life in spite of what happened to her. But her daughter was mentally ill. I once listened to a lecture given by an elderly French psychoanalyst who maintained that it took three generations for mental illness, or psychosis, to develop. I always meant to read more about this theory, but it's tumours, my life's work, that have priority with me: I never get round to reading about anything else.

IT SEEMS THE evening will never end. We have dinner at last: beetroot salad to start with, then calves' liver and mashed potato, with pineapple to follow. Then television and a bit of conversation. When I can keep it up no longer I say I'm going to bed. Petra's convinced there's something seriously wrong with me going to bed before midnight, though she's glad of the chance to doze off herself.

I pretend to sleep and wait for Petra to go to sleep—until she is well and truly asleep. Then I get up, turn on my reading lamp as I sometimes do in the mornings, and look at that beautifully formed head on the pillow, at the glossy black hair on the light-blue pillowcase, at her closed eyes and the shadow of those long eyelashes, and at her mouth, which is so good at kissing.

I long to touch that mouth, long for Petra to touch me and kiss me, on the small of the back, on the shoulder blades, but it's longing and no more. I go through the motions of touching when I touch Petra, and I pretend I'm touched when she touches me, and climax comes and goes as the body requires, but it brings no joy, and it often happens that I weep after leaving her side.

I turn off the lamp, take my clothes from the chair and go into the sitting room. I summon up the will to go out to the car to find the medical report on that girl with the auburn hair, the girl who on a good day could talk to anyone, with her hair cascading fountain-like from the crown of her head, and who would have been so good at caring for others if she'd been given the help she needed.

My farewell letter to Petra falls from my breast pocket as I put on my shirt. What if she were to find the letter before I died? What lie would I have to tell her? That I'd been going to a creative writing class behind her back and that we'd been set the task of writing suicide notes?

That letter should not be in my breast pocket: it's not even in an envelope. I'll have to find a place for it in my briefcase, alongside the auburn-haired girl's medical records. If I find I have no need for it at the weekend it'll go into the shredder in my office. The situation will be clear tomorrow. Tomorrow? What day will that be? What days are these? The days of a life taken up with eliminating tumours, loving Petra after my fashion, living it up with Martin, my soul-mate, running along the city streets at the crack of dawn when half the year round it's dark, and finding myself all of a sudden on my way home from school.

I give thanks for being allowed to exist with Petra, Jadwiga, and Martin, as well as with Mikki of blessed memory, his father and mother and little Petra, and for being allowed to be there for my patients, of whom I'm sincerely fond: my protégés, whose saviour I secretly claim to be.

While giving thanks for all this I'm at odds with my existence as a robot: my soul is tired, it longs for the touch of a healing hand.

Touch is what is wanted, touch, which nothing can replace. Nothing.
Because everything, living and dead, wants to be touched.

The waves make towards the pebbled shore. Hand goes towards hand. Finger towards finger. Mouth towards mouth.

A man untouched is no more than a beast half-dead,
staggering about and pretending he's fully alive.
That's Martin Montag: a sort of ghost,
plodding along in the dark before day begins.

This washout of a man, this sort of ghost, pours rosé wine into a glass before sneaking out to the car to get the auburn-haired girl's medical records. He doesn't understand why he's pouring it, unless its purpose is to tempt him back in again, just in case he goes on some mad drive and takes too long getting home from school: so long a time that it never ends.

He clambers into his shoes as if he's so hung over that he hardly knows his right foot from his left, and steals out. There's no-one about in the cool of midnight apart from MumSomm and DaddyLuft, and they'll stay beside me while I read the medical report on the auburn-haired girl, the girl with that yo-yo fiend of a father. What they now tend to think is that I ought to keep alive and hold onto life, if only for the sake of Petra and Martin, because even though I'm difficult to live with it's better for them that I live than that I don't; and they remind me that I matter a lot to those protégés of mine whom I help to keep on living by attacking the tumours in their bodies with all my might, all my military skill.

Maybe it's that glass of ice-cold rosé, my favourite wine, that has such power of attraction for me that I go back inside instead of going for some crazy drive out into the blue, as my mind is urging me to do. The briefcase feels as heavy as lead in my hand, lengthening my arm. When I'm in the lift I put it down.

As if plagued by a serious illness I settle myself on the sofa under a rug. I take the folded farewell letter from my breast pocket and put it in the briefcase, thus enclosing the end of the world twice in the same briefcase, the farewell letter and the medical report: the end of the world for the auburn-haired girl, which could have been foreseen long since.

I know the words off by heart even though I've locked them in the strongest of strongboxes and thrown away the key: the words about the end of the world for the girl that was, the girl who combed her hair to such effect on the day when her spirits were at their highest. The next day she wept as if she would never stop; I have never heard such weeping before or since. And the day after that she tried to kill herself. She was quite set on it: it was only by chance that she was saved, by a nurse who happened to find her in time.

With the medical report still unopened in my lap I think of Martin and the end of the world for him, in all its multifariousness: lying down to sleep behind a dustbin with the temperature at seven below, a truly decisive step towards ending it all. But he's never told me the reason for it.

THE EIGHTEEN-YEAR-OLD patient, the auburn-haired girl, was alternately aggressive and submissive. The additional dose of tranquilliser that I had to give her had begun to take effect when I spoke to her, but no medicines make any impression on this kind of suffering, neither in standard doses nor additional ones. All the suffering of the world has descended on this one soul. She loses sight of herself as a person and becomes the very picture of suffering.

The drugs made her slur her words, but not even their deadening effect gave her any comfort: she was weeping and wanted to die, to go the same way as her little brother. 'My little brother,' she said, 'who I tried to save from the monster, but there's no way of saving him from the monster. The monster's lying in wait for my little brother. In the passage. In the kitchen. In the sitting room. In the bathroom. In his room. In our parents' bedroom. He's everywhere, the monster. He corners you. He eats into you. Into your brain, into your heart. The monster is a tumour. My beautiful little brother who I tried to look after but just couldn't. He wanted to die. He saw to it himself; and I too must die like him, for the same reason as him. I couldn't protect him. I can't go on living. Help me to die: please let me die, so that I'll never have been born.'

She was an intelligent girl with a good, logical mind. I refrained from pointing out to her that it made no difference how often she died (if indeed it was possible to die more than once): she would still not be able to cancel out the fact of having been born, given that she had indeed been born.

What I should have said to her, if I had been man enough to do so, was that I was fully aware on my own account of this debate about living or not living, being born or not being born, dying or not dying: the debate within myself about whether to be or not to be. It would not have been professional, strictly speaking, and not even a psychiatrist could have presumed to say it; but I was only a medical student. I should have grasped at the one thing that might have had a temporary calming effect on her: the fact that the man behind the desk, the man in the doctor's white coat, was in some sense a fellow-sufferer of hers.

I forced myself to forget the auburn-haired girl and everything to do with her. But as soon as I recognised her at the first floor window of No. 31 I realised I remembered in detail all that had passed between us.

I at once looked up her medical records in the ward, and of course knew them off by heart, right down to the name of her little brother: Heinrich. I remembered that correctly, of course: Heinrich, died aged fifteen. Doctor Steigenstein had taken the trouble to find out for certain that she was telling the truth, at least in this respect: that he had taken his own life, her little brother, at the age of fifteen. He did not believe the reason given for it, though, since in his comments, which I also remembered correctly, he uses the word 'unconvincing'.

It's no easy task measuring the image of a faded ruin of a woman against that of the eighteen-year-old girl who, on her best days, was an adornment to the ward, with a gift for talking to the other patients, cheering them up, and passing the time of day with them. I saw her as the nursing type, as someone who, if we succeeded in helping her, could well become a carer.

She had such beautiful auburn hair. And on days when she was happy she would arrange it in a pony tail at the crown of her head, letting a shimmering stream of hair cascade down to her shoulders. Now she has thin wisps of hair which straggle down to her neck and are clayish in colour. Interesting how the destruction wrought by mental and physical abuse sometimes becomes concentrated in one or another particular place: in the skin of the neck, or on the chin, which may suddenly take on the appearance of old cheese; or in the hair, as in this girl's case.

'MANIC-DEPRESSIVE', SAYS the medical report: they are fantasies, more specifically an elaborate network of fantasies about sexual abuse. It wasn't just from her father that she claimed to have suffered this from the age of four: he had even given one or two friends of his a free hand with her, or was it more than two? And the fantasies also involve her brother, who was supposed to have suffered abuse at their father's hands as well, and to have killed himself for that very reason.

The patient claims that their mother has known about the abuse, but that with her mind damaged after decades of mental and physical violence can do nothing about it. She has secretly pitied the children and spoilt them behind their father's back with sweets and with pocket money which she has somehow scraped together. The patient describes her mother as someone who is dead and her father as a monster. (Senior consultant Doctor Steigenstein sees this as an especially interesting symbolic choice of words, highly indicative of thought adversely affected by a mental illness manifesting itself most clearly in skewed relations with the parents.)

The parents, a respected civil servant and his wife, a housewife, are speechless with grief at the death of their son and at their daughter's mental illness, so dreadful in the form it has taken, with its incrimination of them. They describe their daughter as well-mannered and in general untroubled, saying that it's only when she has her fits that this appalling delusion manifests itself.

A newly qualified psychiatrist, Betti Breitkopf, who took over in the summer break, saw the girl after her attempted suicide in the ward. She writes:

It would be wrong to exclude the possibility that there is some foundation for the girl's accounts of sexual abuse. This *aspect of her case, in my view, needs to be given increased attention as a matter of urgency, and should form a key element in her treatment if found to have a solid basis.*

Shortly afterwards the patient was moved to a private clinic in accordance with her parents' wishes: they considered that with us the girl hadn't been well enough looked after, as the facts of the case showed.

Incredible though it may seem, Doctor Steigenstein discussed the case with me after Betti Breitkopf had put her opinion in writing. I was in my fifth year of studying medicine and the senior consultant was trying out on me a case from his specialist area. He was in a tight spot. So much so that it was better to talk to a novice than to a seasoned colleague. (I have in fact often heard it said that I look as if I'm all-wise: it's the beard, plus the fact that my exam results were legendary.)

The senior consultant was not talking to the right person. This person, not the right one, was careful to say as little as he possibly could to the senior consultant. He stressed that he did not have the terms of reference necessary for assessing the girl's account. On the other hand this same person, not the right one, in the fifth year of his course in medicine, was firmly of the opinion that one should believe a patient rather than not believe a patient, and preferably believe the patient for as long as possible. (I have indeed had good results over time from listening carefully to all that a patient has to say, for example to mysterious descriptions of pains by women of a certain age against whom my colleagues are on their guard, regarding them as hysterical old bats. I can remember at least four of them, strange enough in manner and with strange pains which no run-of-the-mill doctor would have taken seriously. They all survived my treatment, these women, and were cured, though it is true that they remain incurably strange in manner!)

Doctor Steigenstein had been so shocked by the patient's attempted suicide and Betti Breitkopf's view of the case that he was wiping the sweat from his face as we talked. A man whose voice literally trembled.

He said he had been loosely acquainted with the patient's father for a long time. He was an exceedingly charming man, a man of scruples. The alleged abuse was inconceivable: if there was one thing inconceivable about the man, this was it. And the daughter's claim that he had given friends of his a free hand with her virtually proved that it couldn't have happened. It was impossible, was the doctor's refrain. *Impossible.*

I can't imagine which of the two of us was happier when the girl was moved to a private clinic. In my heart of hearts I believed her, and I dearly longed to be of more help to her, but at that point my limits were reached. I was, as I've said, not the right person to be getting involved in this of all cases. I was thoroughly ashamed of my feeble-mindedness and forced myself to wipe from my memory the girl with the auburn hair—who came fully to life again in my mind when I heard that travesty of a laugh at the window of the first floor of No. 31 across the pedestrian street.

And ever since I came home from school the yo-yo man at No. 31 has been walking free, never very far away, and during my time in the psychiatric ward long ago he was so perilously close that I could have run into him in one of the corridors when he came to visit the girl with the auburn hair.

I PUT THE medical report down. I gaze into the candlelight while the crosses on the walls of the room, gliding endlessly by as the headlights pass in the street, turn into the crosses on the graves of MumSomm and DaddyLuft as I read on the wall the questions I must ask.

Am I supposed to heal a monster? Who plays with a bright red yo-yo, tapping it with his index finger, black birthmark and all?

Wouldn't it be better if I did the tapping? If I eliminated the tumour, once and for all?

What sort of method should I use? Devious or direct?

Revenge is not what it's about. I could spend half a century taking revenge and I'd still be coming home from school, when summer was just round the corner. It's about a man lying in wait, intent for as long as he lives on harming a child, and walking free. I've just seen something on the internet about a hundred-year-old paedophile.

Revenge is not what it's about, but because he's found me again, there can be no room on this earth for the two of us.

'I'll kill you if you tell, I'll kill you with an axe.'

He whispered, right into my ear.

Then he handed me the yo-yo and said I could have it. I brushed it aside, but he managed to stick it in my coat pocket as he let me out by the garage door.

There were people out in the street, and those people, whom I didn't know, made me feel it was safe to stay around for a bit. Out here in the street he could do me no harm, he would never be able to harm me again, because now I knew who he was: I could watch out for him.

I sat down, worn out, on the pavement and the sun shone on me, but my face cooled when I'd finished crying and my head froze, and the pain in my body increased as I sat there waiting and saw him come walking along an alleyway. He didn't see me sitting there and I let him get some way along the pavement to where there were some women with prams and a good sprinkling of people. Then I stood up and screamed out:

'I'll tell! I'll kill you!'

He looked round in astonishment and took to his heels. I ran after him, screaming again, more loudly this time:

'I'll tell! I'll kill you!'

He took refuge in a taxi and sat in the back seat with his head in his hairy hands. I saw that he didn't want to be recognised: that he was dead scared.

A woman with a pram came up to me and asked: 'Has he been bothering you, this man?'

The little boy in the pram was waving his dummy and making incomprehensible noises.

I said: 'Yes, he has. Watch out for your child.'

The woman then smiled and I could see that she had understood nothing and that this little boy would one day get bigger and would set off from school, full of the joys of life, and God only knew if he wouldn't stray into the park with no-one having warned him of what could be hiding there.

He was a dear little boy, that boy in the pram, and I do of course sometimes regret that I shall never have a child like him. But however hard I might try there would never be any guarantee of my being able to look after him, or to give him sufficient protection from man-eaters and pirates. My child is best kept eternally unborn for this reason.

I want nothing to do with children, nothing to do with any child. Some of them might be in the grip of appalling suffering under my very nose, without breathing a word, and I wouldn't notice a thing: I wouldn't be able to help.

PETRA IS SLEEPING sweetly, sleeping on her back, and I think of that child of ours who will never come into being—the child she may still desire, for all I know. I still snoop in her make-up bag when she's asleep in the mornings and can see if she's forgotten to take her pill.

I love her most when I watch her sleeping: I empty my mind and become like any other man who's so unbelievably fortunate in loving his wife, and sheer joy rains down over me, joy which keeps me afloat all through the unbearable experience of deriving no feeling from her touch, no feeling from Petra's sweet kisses, kisses which I know are sweet, my mouth knows it, but I can't feel it.

'I'll tell! I'll kill you!' I said. And now he's thrown down the gauntlet after all these years in coming to me with a problem, wanting me to destroy the tumour inside him. I'm in a good position now to keep the solemn promise of my scream: both to tell and to kill him. I can kill myself too, and that's perhaps the very thing I should, in the end, ease my way towards doing, instead of scrubbing myself with a long-handled brush under the shower twice a day in the faint glimmer of the light in the passage, or finding myself when I least expect it on my way home from school and always straying from the homeward route, to where the yo-yo man is hiding in the park by the long water-

fall which is really more like a stream with rapids than a proper waterfall.

IN THE EVENING, when most of the crying had stopped, I came to realise that mother really didn't believe me: there was little point in showing her the yo-yo the man had given me and saying it could be *used in evidence*. Vulgar-minded boys like me should wash their mouths out with soap. Father wasn't listening and my sister didn't believe me, but she wasn't an adult either, she was a teenager. I went to the bathroom, locked myself in, and tried to wash the patch of blood from my underpants. I left them behind on top of the dirty clothes basket and they looked as if mud had been wrung from them—or blood.

Mother came in after I'd got into bed and asked what this muck was on my underpants.

'I've told you,' I said. 'I even showed you the yo-yo he put in my pocket.'

Mother went out and my sister Erna came in and said she was going to read to me.

'I can read alright,' I said. 'There's no need to read to me.'

'I'll read anyway,' said Erna. So she did...

I wept while she was reading, though the book wasn't about anything sad. Erna went out and I heard her saying to mother: 'Martin isn't himself at all.'

'Just keep reading to him,' said mother.

I didn't want Erna around while I was crying so I managed to pull myself together just enough to pretend I was sleeping.

I didn't weep after she had gone. I was destitute, abandoned, alone in the world and hoped I wouldn't wake up the next day. It was as simple as that. If by some mischance I did wake up there were ways I knew of leaving this world. I had come across a novel which gave a detailed description of how to hang yourself. In our garage there was a convenient hook in the ceiling, a workshop table and a wooden crate I could put on the table and kick away once the noose had been tied round my neck and secured with the monkey fist knot, which scoutmaster Rainer said never failed.

I wasn't going to go to school. I'd be sick, would lie in bed until midday, until after mother had gone to work; then I'd go to the garage and hang myself, ideally straight away. Finish it once and for all. Why bother to wait? But killing myself did seem to me a bit hard on Mikki and it occurred to me that I ought to give him some sort of advance warning so that he wouldn't be too devastated when I was dead. That had the drawback, though, that I'd have to put the deed off until after I had spoken to him. And climbing onto the crate on the workshop table would brook no delay.

A SLEEPLESS NIGHT, well rehearsed and often experienced. Martin Montag goes up by the winding staircase to the tower room, taking his laptop with him. He opens the big window and has the impression that the clouds are streaming into the tower along with the moon and the stars, that he is sitting under an open sky, and that there is total silence and absence of sound, like his memory of silence in a Swiss mountain valley. He was seven years old then. A boy who knew his own mind. Not especially cheerful, but certainly not sad. A boy who was puzzling things out all the time, a boy who was just as boys should be.

I turn on the electric heater, switch on the reading lamp, wrap myself in a rug and start surfing the internet in search of news of the latest methods of treatment, in this case for cancer of the oesophagus. My night-time surfing of the internet has sometimes paid off. And this time I happen to find a cocktail of drugs which has worked best in conjunction with radiation on just the kind of tumour that the yo-yo man has. The results of a recent Australian study indicate this clearly.

THE FIRST GLIMMER of daylight nudges at Martin Montag, the insomniac. Maybe he has dozed a bit. He has a job standing up. Needs to get to bed before Petra is up and about.

But she's awake, holding out a hand to him. 'You're cold, right through,' she says.

'I nodded off at the computer. I'm not at all well,' I reply.

And then I remembered all at once that there is such a thing as work, and that I ought to be up already and running along the canal, in the traffic and frantic bustle of the city where the day begins when it's still night. I long to wake up in Istanbul, that megacity of early morning calm. What's the point of being an early riser in a city where the general public drags itself out of bed at the crack of dawn and considers it a virtue to do so? What are all these people doing getting up so early? For me it's different: I positively need to get up early, to be fighting fit, to get a head start on the day.

'There's no way I'll get to work today.'

'This is the first time since we got together that you've not gone to work. Shouldn't I ring for an ambulance?'

'No need for an ambulance. Twenty-four hours should fix it.'

'What exactly is wrong, dearest?'

'Faintness and a splitting headache.'

(Both lies. On the other hand I feel so awful, without being able to give the feeling a specific location, that it seems to me amazing that one can feel like this without dropping down dead.)

'Did you take a pain killer?'

'Yes.'

Petra burrows in under my quilt, placing the whole length of her body alongside mine. She's burning hot. I ought to enjoy feeling the warmth of her body on mine, but it doesn't work like that, not with a deviant like me, all of whose energies are concentrated on not giving voice to his revulsion and not bursting into tears.

How are tears to be explained? Petra has seen me cry on just one occasion, and that was when Effie died. She was an eighteen-year-old patient of mine who ought not to have died: we should have been able to save her. She had a tumour of which seventy-five per cent of patients are cured, but this turned out to be untreatable: a hundred per cent untreatable! When she developed an allergy to the drug that normally works best with radiation the battle was lost.

Effie is not only the most delightful person I have known, but also the most beautiful—a goddess, on a par with Petra and Jadwiga, but a winner even in that company. She had the liveliest of minds like Petra and a mischievous sense of humour like Martin. She was telling jokes on the day she died.

I went to see her just before midday and she told me a joke. I laughed, but she was in too much pain to laugh. Instead I got a lovely smile, meant just for me. I was quite overwhelmed as I returned it, as well I might be, because she had put all her energy into that last smile, meant for me alone. All the charm of the world's most charming person, of my greatest heroine, came together in that smile, on top of the joke. Life is a joke, said the smile, it's absurd, something to smile at, right to the end. None of this is to be taken seriously, we're all going to die and now it's my turn! Yes, mine! I'm smiling at you just to confirm that the whole thing is absurd!

And I laid my hand on the back of hers, marked black and blue by the stabs of the syringe, and she put her other hand on the back of mine and stroked it. And I changed into myself, into me as I was in the Swiss mountain valley, a seven-year-old boy who was able to touch and be touched like a normal person. Ever since Effie touched me I've known what that is like and can call up the memory of it; and in doing so I become the man I was meant to be.

And she spoke these words: *Healing hands.*

Yes, I've been granted the gift of hands that touch gently when treating the sick, as I've often heard people say. Just think! A man with my disability!

I went up to the ward at five to look in on Effie. The nurse saw where I was going and told me that Effie had died.

'But she was telling me a joke only this morning,' I said.

She was an old nurse with steel-grey hair and a steel-grey dental filling. She looked me straight in the eye and asked: 'What joke was that?'

I was suddenly angry. 'Do you expect me to remember that?' I replied.

'Do you wish to see her?' the old witch asked, quite un-abashed.

I made a quick exit and rushed out to the car, still in my white coat. Burst into floods of tears as the lights showed green. Drove like a bat out of hell.

Whether I was in love with Effie I'm not sure, and perhaps that needn't concern me given the way things turned out, but the question remains: what if she had lived?

I fell into Petra's arms when I got home and told her that Effie had died.

Petra tried to comfort me but it was no good, I kept on crying and said that Effie needn't have died. We hadn't gone that extra mile for her.

'Nonsense: you did everything it was humanly possible to do. You couldn't have done more.'

'Yes, but the problem she had is supposed to be curable.'

Petra shook her head and said: 'Now who's talking? Who knows better than you that what's supposed to be curable can't always be cured?'

'But surely it *is* curable? It must be curable! I can't bear it!' (This isn't Martin Montag talking.)

Petra asked if I wanted to see a doctor. 'Are you crazy?' I snapped, and she winced, because I'm usually careful what I say to her and how I say it. I added that she knew better than anyone that the only doctor I could think of going to see was myself. The embarrassment of running blubbing to a colleague would be unbearable!

In the end Petra suggested that I took a sleeping pill even though it was only nine o'clock. I did, and went out like a light. When I awoke around two in the morning I had to acknowledge that all was not well with my nerves. I wondered for a whole week whether I ought to change jobs. I had after all once thought of becoming a vet.

I aired this possibility with Petra. She didn't dismiss it (as any other wife would surely have done), but discussed with me the pros and cons of such a new dimension to my life.

'But your patients are tremendously lucky to have you', she volunteered, at one stage in our conversation.

These simple words at once set me back on track. (As if I hadn't known all along that my patients were damn lucky!). I abandoned the vet idea for the time being.

'You must never again become so deeply attached to a patient,' she said. 'Never.'

'I know, I know, I know.'

So I let Effie be a lesson to me. Until I met my friend Martin. If I had lost him, I would have lost myself as well. I would have gone straight down the chute after him.

Then dear Petra strokes me on the cheek, gets up, covers me with a blanket and urges me to go to sleep, which is what I yearn for, the world's longest sleep, in the absence of sound, in the Swiss mountain valley, when I was seven years old. When time should have stood still but did not; instead it rushed forward like a train on inevitable rails and failed to deliver me from evil when we stopped over at the next station. Alone and abandoned by all mankind, delivered unto evil. And with no hope of succour. Except indirectly, among foreigners in Berlin where there was life and joy and a symphony of colours and smells and a place where I didn't mind them touching me because they were different from us and not the same colour as that fiend with the yo-yo or my mother and father who didn't believe me when my life depended on it, and instead betrayed their child then and for ever.

After having a cup of coffee, Petra comes in and offers to ring the hospital for me to let them know I'm not well. I feel so wretched that I let her do it, and remain basking in her warmth, aching all over, and nowhere so much as in my sleepless eyes.

The secretary Petra speaks to has worked for us for two years. It's high time I got a grip on myself and started remembering her name without effort: it's not enough to remember that something like *Ja* is someone's name. When I say the name I say that much and swallow the rest: 'Frau Ja...', I say. Her name is Jahr, German for 'year': Edeltraut Jahr, Frau Jahr, Mrs Jahr. I must never forget it. Edeltraut Jahr, Frau Jahr.

Frau Jahr (not 'Ja'!), is one of the invisible staff, working behind the scenes. She works silently and without fuss. With none of the hustle and bustle I've come to expect of the hospital. I can't get used to the German work ethic, having been brought up by parents who never made their hard work obvious, getting through it quickly while seeming to work slowly. That's how I go about things. I'm told I never look as though I'm in a hurry, when in fact I'm constantly rationing my time, always working at the greatest possible speed.

A shaft of morning light thrusts its way through the flaps of the curtains. I ask dear Petra to cover the window completely.

'I daren't risk going to work,' she says, startled. 'You literally can't raise your head from your pillow.'

'There's nothing seriously wrong with me, nothing serious,' I say, in desperation (at the thought of being stuck with her, at not being left alone). Then I say: 'If I really need help, Martin is free today: we were going to meet after work and I could easily ask him round. But it won't be necessary: I'll just doze off.'

'Has something happened?' she asks in low tones, a slight tremor in her voice.

'Something's always happening,' I reply.

'It's body and soul with you, isn't it? There's no better doctor than you are. I sometimes think that for you work is both body and soul. But it also makes life inhumanly difficult for you.'

'I can think of no alternative. For me it's a matter of life and death, of mortal combat. I wouldn't be doing it otherwise.'

'Then do as other mortals do: get the support of professionals in facing your difficult tasks.'

'You mean psychotherapy?'

'That or something like it. From a good psychiatrist.'

'Or perhaps become a vet, letting the psychiatrist off the hook?'

'My dearest husband, I wish I knew what was best for you.' And she leans over and kisses my cheek, her hair tickling my ear.

'How fortunate I am,' I say in a voice that comes out clear, albeit from a state of utter exhaustion: 'How fortunate I am.'

'Make the most of it, then, my darling.'

And she strokes my arms which are lying on top of the quilt. The crazy notion enters my head that my arms are dead while the rest of me is still pulsating. Best not to put it to the test until after Petra has gone.

She brings a bottle of water, a glass and a banana and puts them down on my bedside table. She gets the phone and puts it there as well.

'I'll ring you when I've got into work,' she says.

'No, don't do that, I may be asleep. Let me ring you instead.'

'Well, if you haven't rung by eleven, I'll ring you.'

'My dearest love, my one true love,' I say, and try to enunciate the words like a singer of *Lieder*, in case they should be the last she ever hears me say.

Petra shuts the door behind her and I try moving my arms. They're not dead, it seems. So the whole of Martin is alive! For how much longer?

DEATH BY ONE'S OWN HAND

Anyone who thinks that 'death by one's own hand' is a simple matter is under a misapprehension. Pragmatism, courage, and considerable strength of character are required to bring it about. Suicide does not come easily to the faint-hearted. Pills may be taken, it is true, provided that swallowing presents no difficulties, but this approach is not without risk: pill suicides are all too often found to retain the vital spark, and are then resuscitated, to their great anger and distress, so that the whole process has to be repeated.

A key question is WHERE? *Someone with relatives who is contemplating suicide needs to consider the question of who will find the body, hence the question: Where?*

If the potential suicide is a family man and of sufficiently sound mind he will see to it that his child does not find his body. If not, he will perform the act of suicide wherever he happens to be at the time. His need for release will be paramount, however great the difficulties (and no matter who may find him).

Finding a place for the act is a more complicated matter than the act itself. If the person intent on dying is still sufficiently in command of his faculties he will be careful not to choose a remote location for his suicide, since this will add uncertainty to the distress that his relatives will inevitably suffer if he vanishes without trace and cannot be found for days afterwards, or even longer.

So the key question, once again, is WHERE? Suggestions gratefully received.

IN DEFIANCE OF the law of gravity and several other laws I make it: into the shower, into my clothes, and down the stairs. It's amazing how unattractive the lift now seems to a runner who, with feet of clay, at last has need of it. And those feet of clay even think, bless them, that they can function out in the street.

The car takes me to my parents' house. I haven't been round there since Christmas. Our fir tree by the garage, like something from Grimms' fairy tales, was then as white as snow, with a little bird sitting in it, screeching away in ear-splitting tones as if to convey its utter contempt for cards displaying White Christmases like this. Petra and I burst out laughing and the wretched bird fell silent.

The tree was of manageable dimensions when I was little. It's so big these days and draws such attention to itself that you can hardly see into the garage. In my old room it creates an eternal darkness, and its self-importance is such that tampering with it is an actionable offence.

But the place has been found. It was within view all the time, of course, though I pretended not to see it. The solution, too, has been found, the answer to the question WHERE? The word *garage* gives the answer, and the man seeking it has had the foresight to bring the key with him from home, where he has always kept it in a special place.

The key inevitably fits the lock, and inevitably the door opens, and the table is waiting in readiness, as it has always done, from the very first day, and the hook in the ceiling is still exactly where it has always been.

The apparatus envisaged in the old days is no longer necessary. There's no need for a crate on the workshop table: the table is now the right height. The whole process will be so much easier for a thirty-four-year-old man of six foot two than for an eight-year-old boy. The grown man won't need a crate to reach up to the hook, and he'll be strong enough with those marathon-trained legs of his to kick the whole table away from under him.

The only questions now remaining are at what TIME and on which DAY? There must be no-one at home. Weekends are no good. The day will have to be a Monday, a Wednesday, or a Friday, when mother's working after midday. It's actually Friday today. A good day on which to hang oneself. With Effie's poem as a guiding light?

Life is not
held fast in my hand.

I can hold on no longer: it is life's wish
that I let go

as those who went before me all did in the end.
Even those who had a firmer hold than mine.

THE ROUTE IS via the park which I have avoided every day since the time when I was coming home from school and looked at my reflection in the pond on my way to the waterfall, where I was planning to dip my toes.

There's a cherry tree in full blossom leaning over the pond and looking at itself in the water. The eternity of narcissism thus makes a perfect postcard. But the perfect peace of the scene is not left in peace, for a small boy has appeared with a performance that intrudes on the still life of eternity. He picks the blossoms from the tree and throws them, handful after handful, into the pond, where the petals swim sweetly on reflected wisps of cloud, so that heaven and earth run together in the water.

'Heaven and earth, MumSomm. There's nothing to separate them any more: they're side by side, heaven and earth, as you can see in the water. It's the rollercoaster for me now: I'll reach you in no time. There's nothing to it, as scoutmaster Rainer always said.'

The flower boy looks up and lets his eye settle on this Martin Montag, who is talking to himself.

'Now let's see,' says Mummy Sommer. 'Isn't there some time in hand?'

She's never said this before, and I answer in surprise: 'Yes, there is time in hand. Isn't that just the trouble?'

'Time and time. Trouble and trouble,' she says.

As in the beginning of 'The Radiologist's Lament':

Time is time and trouble is trouble
and trouble is time and time is trouble,
and that's just the trouble: that time is trouble...

In the next glade I come to, there looms before me a tree of amazingly blue colour, just like the ones in those paintings: who was it again who was always painting blue trees? I have no idea what that kind of tree is called, and it's maddening, not being able to remember the name of that painter of blue trees.

A bald man in a light-coloured suit comes walking towards me, and I bid him good day and say I want to know the name of this fantastically blue tree. He cannot help me, unfortunately, even though he's a great admirer of everything that grows: he's never allowed himself the time to make a study of trees or remember their names, but some day he will, he adds. I say the same, feeling half ashamed of myself for not having attended a course on trees. I can't understand why not, as I love them so much. I can't understand it, I repeat with emphasis. The man is suddenly in a hurry and says goodbye. I turn round, walking in the same direction as him, and the man looks back, his eyes popping.

The trees sway in the wind, ripples appear in the pond, a whirlwind of cherry blossom hits the water and the boy by the tree starts laughing and the sun laughs too, with gusto. I cross the street to the pavement opposite and stuff myself with the fullest of full breakfasts: ham, scrambled egg, chipolatas, mustard, fried potatoes, toast, cheese and orange marmalade, not finishing until I've also had a couple of macchiatos. I read the *Kreuzberg Chronicle* with one eye and glance sideways at the waterfall with the other, watching the sun disport itself in the gleaming rush of water, and I see in the paper that there's a Japanese cherry blossom festival in the park today, beginning at five. The idea is to look at the blossoms on the trees and the ones that have fallen to the ground. (What about the ones on the pond?) We're advised to take rugs and the paper tells you where you can buy picnic baskets, which I already knew anyway, from when it was Petra's birthday: I took her on a surprise picnic trip with a well-filled basket, not saying where to, and she jumped for joy when the bottle of ice-cold champagne was opened by the pond in the wood which I know so well from going on Sunday nature walks with mother and father. I really ought to surprise my friend Martin by getting us a picnic basket so that we could embark on a systematic viewing of the blossoms: what they call *hanami*, 'flower-viewing', in Japanese, according to the paper.

A whole cast of weird characters sails past. An elderly man in an electrically powered wheelchair zooms by, fooling with a woman on his lap, laughing wildly, and only just missing my toes. A man with a beard reaching below his waist approaches on a bicycle, his beard held in check by a long succession of elastic bands. As he passes me I see that he has only one arm. Here's a test for the one-armed: see if you can get twenty rubber bands round your beard!

Martin Montag, the main character in this film about his own life, is so involved in the contemplation of these oddballs that he finishes breakfast and stops reading the paper, overwhelmed by a sense of the Felliniesque character of human life, and at a loss to understand why Berliners bother with the theatre or the cinema. No director in the world could have invented these people on the pavement, least of all the seventy-year-old man who's walking at a rapid pace on the other side of the street and going into elaborate dance positions at every fifth step. And who, I wonder, gives this dancer so much as a sidelong glance? Not a soul. It's simply part of the city's daily routine: free entertainment as a matter of course, all day and every day. A little woman in a trench coat comes walking towards the dancer and bows to him. He gives a loud bray of laughter and the woman continues on her way with clacking footsteps, in her impenetrable battledress.

I'm sitting at the wheel when I realise that I forgot to pay. I go back and confess my crime. The waiter, a young man with an altogether delightful manner, just smiles and says all is now in order. His eyes are bright with the joy of life, and the hands that give me my change have long artistic fingers. I ask him if he's an artist and indeed he is: he paints, and has held one private viewing of his paintings. I say I'd like to follow his work and ask for his card, which he is happy to give me, and I tell him my name's Martin and give him as much of a tip as I feel I can without looking ridiculous, shake him by his artistic hand, say a fond goodbye and wish him good luck.

Stravinsky's *Rite of Spring* assails me on all sides from those crazy loudspeakers which I arranged at great expense to have fitted in my car after having the original ones removed, even though they were more than adequate. Petra and I saw *The Rite of Spring* performed by the Bolshoi Ballet at the Paris Opéra. It was the experience of a lifetime, which we recall again and again: the fiercely beautiful music and the death dance of the sacrificial maidens. A riot broke out at the Paris premiere in 1913 and the dancers had to run for their lives. But where is the nearest shop with books about trees coming to blossom in spring? Wouldn't you like to have been a fly on the wall, dear Martin keeps asking, when Stravinsky met Debussy in the street in Paris with the music of *The Rite of Spring* under his arm, and said he'd arranged it for four hands? Debussy and Stravinsky dashed into the nearest piano bar and played *The Rite of Spring* right through. Wouldn't you like to have been a fly on the wall? Wouldn't you? You would think that Martin Martinetti's greatest regret in life was to have missed those two composers playing *The Rite of Spring* in that piano bar. His mad insistence on this was such that I felt I had to remind him that he hadn't even been born then.

'No, I wasn't born then, more's the pity: the greatest of pities,' he said with such deadly seriousness that I didn't know what to think.

Half-way through *The Rite of Spring* my car sails into the Steinplatz. A favourite bookshop of mine is close by. It's not too large but large enough. I first went there with father when he was buying books on carpentry, or those books on Switzerland which we read from cover to cover before going there.

The blonde with her hair up who works in the shop is wearing a close-fitting black dress of soft material which reaches down to below her knees. What a sucker I am for blonde hair worn up like that! I gaze spellbound at the perfect Jadwiga-style knot tied in that perfectly blonde hair.

I sometimes visit the shop and have seen this woman before, but I've never noticed till now what beautiful legs she has, how elegantly curved her calves are, how slender her ankles, how arched each instep! She's wearing low-heeled, beige-coloured, patent leather shoes. The very picture of elegance and beauty, and the manner to go with it! I'm keen to know her name, and there it is on her badge: Stefanie Schulz. I'd put her somewhere between forty-five and sixty years old.

I call her Frau Schulz and she is no way put out by such

a personal form of address, offering to help me find books, and I tell her I'm looking for two books on trees coming to blossom, one large and one of pocket size, and Stefanie Schulz looks straight into my eyes—which is possible, even with my beard in the way—and it strikes me that I could easily see myself touching this woman. A first, if ever there was one! She could be my mother. But she just isn't.

She has earrings that glisten with much the same colour as the dark blue tree in the park. She speaks in gently modulated tones and her voice is wonderfully clear: the laughter in her voice is like a Frenchwoman's. Perhaps she sings in a choir, perhaps she's an actress. She has a perfect figure, with her elegant shoulders, slender waist and long thighs. Her age shows itself in the wrinkles round her eyes, but Stefanie Schulz is far from having shed her beauty. I play at touching her little finger as I pay her and she plays at touching the back of my hand when she gives me the books. These micro-touches trigger off currents of feeling that I cannot recognise from any previous state of existence. I've even reached the point of wondering whether she might perhaps like to sleep with me—if I first got rid of the beard.

She smiles when I say goodbye. A lovely smile. I'd like to see a photo of her when she was thirty. It's all I can do not to say this out loud. I'm passionately in love with Stefanie Schulz. Will that make her happy? Maybe just a bit.

Out in the street I'm alone in the world, away from such sophisticated beauty. There can be no doubt that a woman

who looks like that will be fond of *Lieder*. I'd like to listen
to Schubert's *Winterreise* with her. A modest enough wish,
with no complications. Not too much to ask, surely, in the
course of one life? I could carry on working on this tomorrow: go to the shop, buy something on Schubert, and
start a conversation. It would be a simple matter for me to
ease into the shop again as early as tomorrow. There would
be an opportunity on the way to my mother-in-law or on
the way back. But perhaps Stefanie Schulz doesn't work on
Saturdays. No, of course she doesn't work on Saturdays.
She'll be spending all her weekends listening to Schubert
in a robe reaching to her feet that's been specially made in
Thailand, with a scarf of natural silk round her neck because her voice is so important to her. I'll bet she also goes
out for walks with her little dog, or she wouldn't be so well
preserved—always with a good scarf on, so that the wind
doesn't get to her throat.

It's tempting to tell Martin about Stefanie Schulz. That
Frenchman understands everything. But the humorist in
him would find it too funny. This Martin, Martin Montag, would be making himself the target of embarrassing
jokes about mother complexes erupting in the bookshop
and proliferating.

The pocket-sized book that I've just bought is called *The
Little Book of Flowering Trees*.

The botanical gardens. There can't be many people about
now among those fairytale trees, sprayed with blue paint

by some hyperactive magician. How would it be to take the book along and ask those who know about these things what the different kinds of trees are, and put a mark by each one?

I go to the car and leave the large book there. I take with me *The Little Book of Flowering Trees* and walk in the direction of the lake. In spring and autumn when the temperature's nice and warm, say twenty degrees Celsius, I go along the paths by the lake for my Sunday morning marathon. I'm actually pretty fussy about the temperature, even though I make myself run in more or less any weather, though I draw the line at anything more than ten below or twenty-seven above. I can run well enough in the coldest and hottest of weathers, but I feel it would be a touch fanatical to go out running in more than ten below or twenty-seven above. I don't want to be that sort of person. There were such temperature swings one year that I missed thirty-one morning runs. Thirty-one! A whole month, for goodness' sake!

It's a pleasure to go running and a pleasure to skip a run. But it's no use letting the pleasures occur at random. You need to prepare. To see what temperature is forecast before you go to sleep. If running's not on I set my alarm at fifteen minutes later than usual, and in the morning I drink one more cup of coffee than custom demands and make some toast: toasted white bread, that is, with butter (plenty of it: I can't stand thinly spread butter) and orange marmalade: as gluttonously good to eat as it is bad for you. When I retire I plan to have toast every single morning, with lots of butter and orange marmalade. Oh, alright then, every other morning.

The last time I was here was in October, but only now do I notice the colours of autumn. They were all around me then as I ran, but they made no impression on me as I sped blindly on my way. Now I recreate those vanished colours in all their glory. What the magic spray gun produces in spring is no match for them.

I sit down for a moment on a bench that I know of old and the swan sails by beneath the branches of the weeping willow, leaving a long trail behind it in the water and bowing its head to me, while the world's entire population of dogs scampers by in the highest of canine spirits, with their owners following behind. Just think of the number of people whom no-one understands except their dog, and how many things there are that no-one knows, but your dog does! The dog, the all-knowing, the comforter: a hymn with its own tune.

Half-way through lunch it dawns on me that I've already had breakfast, but I still wolf down my favourite Turkish delicacies with ravenous hunger and make a show of myself in the restaurant by inflicting my smattering of the language on the Ottoman goddess who's serving me—and serving me with such grace that I can only assume she's a third-generation belly-dancer.

It's not unknown for patients to have an insatiable appetite on the last day of their lives. There are supposed to be chemical reasons for this, which I've never found very convincing. I think it has to do with the sense that this is the last day left to us in which to enjoy our food.

One of my perkiest patients, George Franklin, ended his life in exactly that spirit. He was a man of fifty who never let bad news affect him, but whose medical history was one continuous string of bad news. Everything was always worse than it seemed to be at first. The main tumour had pushed further into the abdominal wall than we thought. And there were metastases that were not spotted soon enough. He lived only four months after his problem was diagnosed, rather than the two years we told him he could hope for.

One morning, after having been semi-conscious for days on end, he sat up in bed and said: 'What sort of a hospital is this? Has breakfast been abolished?'

It was just after ten, and the breakfast trolleys had come and gone, but a nurse who was especially fond of him and knew what he liked to eat nipped out and got him a cappuccino and some chocolate croissants.

By three o'clock he was dead, and the nurse who was especially fond of him wept as she told his wife that he had woken up hungry and asked what was going on, whether breakfast had been abolished at this hospital, and that she had broken the rules and nipped out to get him some breakfast. And the two of them wept together at the thought of George Franklin's last breakfast, holding hands for a long time in the day room, the nurse repeating many times that he had sat up, drunk his coffee, eaten a couple of chocolate croissants and then died.

I PARK THE car by the wall of my churchyard. I go over in my mind the content of the farewell letter which I've known by heart for a long time apart from line three: *A chance incident at work...*, and which I finally got down to writing. It's a rotten letter: a communication that raises questions, but gives no answers, and it's also written in a scrawl that makes it look as if I'm parodying a doctor's illegible handwriting on a prescription. But I must leave this behind rather than nothing at all: I've no choice here.

Petra, my dearest darling,

I have failed you.
I've concealed from you as well as I could the fact that I'm only half a man.
A chance incident at work has made it impossible for me to go on living.

Something has happened which has rendered me utterly incapable.

But half a man can love with his whole heart and soul, and I do. I am more fortunate than words can express in having shared with you my days and nights. And I am, in spite of everything, happier to have been born than not to have been. That is entirely due to you.

But now I can cope no longer. As time goes on, or even sooner, you will be better off without me.

Please forgive me. Forgive me. I've been sailing under false colours. I longed to exist as a man, and with you most of all, and I tried, but it just wasn't possible.

Your Martin.

In the glove compartment I find an envelope for the letter. I hide it for the moment in the back under the mat, behind the driver's seat.

This farewell-letter-writer-cum-viewer-of-flowers carries the picnic baskets over the street, hoping he cuts a reasonable figure.

I put the baskets down by the coffee-table, lean back in the sofa and look at them. It would be better to put the gravlax and dill sauce in the fridge, if there's going to be a delay with the flower-viewing, but I stay where I am.

A long ray of sunlight from the tower window is lying across the floor of the living room. Let's hope it stays there for as long as possible and supports me in what needs to be done.

What urgently needs to be done. I have to treat a man who is a tumour himself, a spreader of cancers, who killed his son and reduced his daughter to a total wreck. How many others has he ruined with that toy of his?

I'm a fighting man. My role in life is to kill tumours. It's as simple as that. But finding the best ways of doing it requires careful thought.

I MUST HAVE left the door open, because I don't hear it when he arrives, and don't see him until he's standing there in front of me by the coffee-table, looking at me and away from me, at the baskets.

'Hello,' I say.

'Hello,' he says, remaining standing where he is.

'How about a spot of flower-viewing?' I say.

'Why not?'

And Martin sits down facing me. He doesn't take off his jacket or shoes, any more than his host has done.

'Flower-viewing is called *hanami* in Japanese,' I say.

'Yes,' he replies.

'It starts at five.'

'At five.'

'Yes, five. But we can of course go when we like.'

'Of course.'

It's not unusual for pauses to occur in my conversations with Martin, so I don't notice the silence until he says all at once:

'One basket each?'

'We can't do with less,' I reply.

'No,' he says.

And suddenly I blurt it out, quite involuntarily, my new secret.

'I want to listen to *Winterreise* with Stefanie Schulz, the woman in the bookshop, Frau Schulz. I bought some books from her about flowering trees.'

'How very poetic of you!'

'I even want to touch her, and that's a first!'

'You even want to touch her, and that's a first?'

'Yes.'

'You're teetering on the verge of telling me something. Something new!'

'Well, she's old. Fifty maybe, or even forty-five. Maybe sixty.'

'That doesn't count as old in France. Fifty-year-old women in France are still women at that age, and later.'

'The French are always one step ahead. Except when it comes to Shakespeare. They just don't get Shakespeare, the world's greatest writer. I've never understood that.'

'What do you know about Shakespeare?'

'Oh, this and that.'

'Why have you never talked to me about Shakespeare before?'

'He's for me to keep to myself. He's not for the market-place.'

'I didn't know I was a marketplace.'

'I just can't get my head round this problem the French have with Shakespeare.'

'They naturally don't understand his sense of humour. And there's something superficial about them as a nation, perhaps.'

'I'm not having you talking about the French like that. There's no-one so sophisticated as a Frenchman.'

'It's possible to be superficial as well as sophisticated, as a French snob like you should know.'

'I sometimes wonder what it is you have against your own country.'

'I'm now half Polish, thank goodness, so it makes a difference which country you're talking about. But anyone with half a brain of course has something against his own country. The better you know something, the more its faults stare you in the face, whether it's a person or a country.'

'You're in philosophical mode today.'

'That's more than can be said for you. What's the explanation of that look on your face?

'What do you mean? That I'm unshaven?'

'I'm not talking about that Stone Age beard of yours or

your mop of hair, but those wild eyes glaring at me from under those Stone Age eyebrows.'

'I'm tired.'

'That's pretty obvious. What's making you tired?'

'I need to kill someone.'

'Isn't it a bit premature being tired before the murder's done?'

'I didn't get enough sleep. What kept me awake was the question of what method to use. It's the method that's the problem. The rest is child's play.'

'Can I be of any help?'

'I didn't know you were experienced in such things.'

'Murder interests me, as you know. I'm a great reader of thrillers.'

'Well, the question is whether I do it pat, just like that, or by medical means. And it's a moral question as well as a technical one.'

'I would never have dreamt that any human being could have such an effect on you that you'd go to the trouble of killing them.'

'Now there's a thought,' I reply.

'Unless it was yourself, or Petra.'

'Yes, or you.'

'I'm honoured. So who's to be killed?'

'A patient.'

'A patient?'

'Yes.'

'That's an unusual approach for a doctor.'

'True enough. Perhaps I should be killing myself instead.'

'That would be more in line with the Hippocratic oath.'

'Indeed.'

'Or you could do both, as long as you forgot about Hippocrates and remembered to do them in the right order.'

'I know. That was one of my ideas.'

'Why not count up to ten? Wait till after the weekend. Wait till after your birthday. That's on Monday.'

'I know it's on Monday. Do you think I'm completely out of touch? And what difference does it make dying at thirty-four rather than thirty-five.'

'Good question.'

'I've got everything ready for the off. Farewell letter and all.'

'May I see it?'

'It's not here. It's in the car. Under the mat.'

'Why don't we make a pact? You get to see my farewell letter if I get to see yours?'

'Are you honestly keeping that down-and-out letter of yours for future use?'

'I always carry it with me to remind me of life.'

'You carry a suicide note with you to remind you of life?'

'Yes. Perhaps I should let you have it to remind you of the same thing.'

Martin takes a crumpled envelope from his breast pocket and waves it in my face. Sure enough, it's addressed to Mad-

ame Agathe Martinetti, in Antibes, France. To my intense
discomfiture he tears open the envelope and hands me the
letter.

'Oh no,' I say, looking away.

'I'll read it to you if you like,' says Martin.

I don't like to refuse, so Martin starts reading, in strong,
decisive tones, just like Dietmar Sonnenschein the weather
man, a great favourite of Martin's and mine.

Dear Aunt Agathe,

*This is a thank-you letter, even though I'm at loss to know
how to begin to thank you. As a child I knew only one grown-
up person on whom I could rely, a person with her wits fully
about her, who understood me and my circumstances, and
that, of course, was you. (There was a certain housemaid as
well, perhaps, but she was a maid.) Without having known
you I wouldn't have had a scrap of faith in humankind and
wouldn't have lived the life I have up to now.*

*I'll no longer be alive when you read this letter, but I want-
ed to be sure that you knew how things had turned out for
me. I feel nothing but warmth when I think of you, and that
has served me well, I can tell you, given my station in life—
especially in the winters!*

Wishing you health and happiness, dearest Aunt Agathe,

> *your devoted*
> *Martin*

'Don't say anything, that's just how it is,' says Martin, immediately after reading the letter.

'But I wasn't going to say anything.'

'That's typical of your apathy.'

'I'll need at least a year to digest it.'

'In the meantime you could perhaps tell me what's got into you.'

'It's an old secret.'

'Maybe you're talking to the right person.'

'How so?'

'I'm in my element with old secrets.'

'Hardly with ones like mine.'

'You never know,' he says, with a smile.

I'm tempted to ask my friend to wipe that smile off his face, but I don't want to be guilty of offending him when he's not only made a point of coming to see me, but has actually taken his own suicide note from its sealed envelope and read it to me. So I wait in sullen silence until he asks:

'What did he do to you, this man, when you were small?'

'How do you know it was a man, and that he did something, and that I was small?'

'Elementary, my dear Watson. You said it was an old secret, so you can't have been very old at the time. It's usually men who do things to children and he must have harmed you pretty badly for you to want to kill him.'

'He did. He raped me.'

'How often?'

'What do you mean, how often?'

'I mean: how often?'

'Once.'

'Well, you got off pretty lightly compared with some children.'

I raise my hand to strike my friend across the cheek, but it freezes within a hair's-breadth of his jaw.

'Got off lightly?!' I shout. 'What kind of friend are you? What kind of low-lifer would say that? That a child was raped and got off lightly?!'

'If it's raped just once then it does get off lightly compared with a child who's been raped every day for as long as it can remember, until it's seven years old. With one exception: on New Year's Day, when it was still only six.'

'What in God's name are you talking about?'

'Do you mean who am I talking about?'

'No, what? What's this about New Year's Day being an exception, and a six-year-old child?'

'Well, that was the day he left me alone. He killed himself on New Year's Day the following year.'

'Who, for Christ's sake?'

'My father, of course.'

'Your own father?'

'Who else?'

'Oh Martin, my dear friend, forgive me! I had no idea.'

'You know what? I think we often do have an idea but just don't know we have it.'

'My dear friend, what was it that happened to you?' I ask, like an idiot, because he's already told me what happened, and the tears gush from me in a never-ending flow, pouring like hail into my lap as I cry even more than when Effie died. I've never cried like this in my life before, except once, on the day when I was coming home from school.

'The same thing happened to you as to me, except that you were murdered once and for me it was a thousand times. And for me it was actually him: not a stranger.'

'Lisa,' I manage to say.

'You're crying so much that I can't understand what you're saying.'

'LISA. The scarecrow. The auburn-haired girl that was. Her name is Lisa. I've always remembered it, though I pretended to forget it.'

'So it's her father?'

'The monster lying in wait for her little brother. In the passage. In his room. In the bathroom.'

'Your patient, you mean?'

'Yes. He's swallowed a yo-yo.'

'What?'

'That's what it looks like. The tumour. He had a yo-yo

with him when I came home from school. Now at last I can kill him. I said I would when I screamed at him.'

'Leave it for a bit. You're in no state to be killing anyone today. Not even yourself.'

I take my friend in my arms, still crying, and he starts crying and puts his arms round me, and the two of us tremble together uncontrollably until I disengage myself from his frantic grip. I go to the bathroom and throw up, retching so much that I think I'm going to sick up my liver and lungs.

When I stagger back into the sitting room Martin is no longer crying. He sponges my face, gives me some water, and wipes away the traces of vomit on the collar of my suede jacket. I ask him to stop: the jacket's ruined. My favourite jacket! On the other hand there's some cheese, tuna salad, gravlax and dill sauce still in the picnic baskets, in danger of going off. Could he possibly put them in the fridge?

He does as I ask, then leads me into the bedroom, takes off my suede jacket, and settles me in the marital bed. I lie there like an all-time weakling, without the slightest interest in whether I'm going to live or die.

But I do manage to say: 'Come and lie beside me, my friend, so that I don't die.'

'We're not going to die yet. Not now, after coming all this way.'

He lies down beside me and takes me in his arms. I lie

with his arms right round me and I can't understand it: I'm supposed to have a horror of being touched. And haven't I also signed my own death warrant? But I'm happy enough for the moment to have someone take me in their arms; there's comfort in that.

AND TWO LITTLE boys, who after the battle had staggered about on the battlefield, now go to sleep, wounded and worn out, and when they wake up they are not healed of their harms, it is true, but they are rested, and are gleefully surprised, even glad, to have survived what has fallen to their lot; and it's still broad daylight and the birds are in such high spirits that their exuberant song is almost overdone, and the sun, not to be left out, joins in the fun, teasing most especially the leaves on the twin trees that shelter the graves of Sommer and Luft.

For more information or to receive our newsletter,
please contact us at: info@worldeditions.org.